Damosel

In Which the Lady of the Lake Renders a Frank and Often Startling Account of her Wondrous Life and Times

STEPHANIE SPINNER

Alfred A. Knopf

New York

For Karina, Nathaniel, Dyllan, and Rachel

THIS IS A BORZOI BOOK PUBLISHED BY ALFRED A. KNOPF

Visit us on the Web! www.randomhouse.com/teens

Educators and librarians, for a variety of teaching tools, visit us at www.randomhouse.com/teachers

Library of Congress Cataloging-in-Publication Data
Spinner, Stephanie.
Damosel : in which the Lady of the Lake renders a frank and often startling account of her wondrous life and times / Stephanie Spinner. — 1st ed.
p. cm.
Summary: Damosel, a rule-bound Lady of the Lake, and Twixt, a seventeen-year-old dwarf, relate their experiences as they strive to help King Arthur face Morgause, Morgan, and Mordred, one through her magic and the other through his humble loyalty.
ISBN 978-0-375-83634-3 (trade) — ISBN 978-0-375-93634-0 (lib. bdg.)
1. Lady of the Lake (Legendary character)—Juvenile fiction. [1. Lady of the Lake (Legendary character)—Fiction. 2. Dwarfs—Fiction. 3. Fools and jesters—Fiction. 4. Arthur, King—Fiction. 5. Magic—Fiction. 6. Knights and knighthood—Fiction. 7. Great Britain—History—To 1066—Fiction.] I. Title.
PZ7.S7567Dam 2008
[Fic]—dc22
2007043519

The text of this book is set in 11-point Giovanni Book.

Printed in the United States of America

October 2008

10 9 8 7 6 5 4 3 2 1

First Edition

Contents

A Lady Always Keeps Her Promises.

—from *The Rules Governing the Ladies of the Lake*

PART ONE

In Which Damosel Fashions a Sword

I am so well versed in *The Rules Governing the Ladies of the Lake* that I could recite them backward on a dare, but the wisdom I treasure most was gleaned not from that vast, ancient compendium, but from my own earnest blundering. To wit: learn the Rules so you know when to break them.

It took me half a lifetime to understand this.

Long ago I had no inkling. I was a feckless young lake spirit, living in damp contentment in a place called Looe Pool. My home was deep and wide, the limpid blue of an aquamarine. Because it was only a stone's throw from the ocean, I could hear waves breaking day and night—a steady, soothing sound, like a giant breathing through a stuffy nose.

Grand as the ocean was, nothing compared to my Lake, for its water was refreshing in summer, bracing in winter, and, unlike the surf, very drinkable. I loved its taste of ducks' feet and shale.

I treasured solitude in those days, so I kept the Lake hidden. It was a feat well within my powers, for as a Lady, I commanded significant magic, just as my forebears had. There are severe restrictions to what I can divulge ("A Lady Does Not Discuss Her Ancestry or Her Training"), but I will say that I could obscure most things (including myself) to mere shadows and could move from one element to another as smoothly as rain gliding off a leaf. Like other Ladies, I knew countless helping and hindering spells, and I need hardly mention that I was bewitching, with every sort of glamour at my disposal—from the subtler ones all the way up to the dizzying, the blinding, and the stupefying.

Moreover, I could see what was hidden in men's hearts—which had its advantages, as men are always trying to hide something. But it was a gift I seldom used, for in those days I avoided mortals, deeming them rough, hasty creatures with indifferent manners and unfathomable customs. They were boistous, too—noisier than birds but without the pretty feathers. So I kept my distance, and they kept their secrets.

Another of my talents (and an unusual one for a Lady) was the ability to work metal, which I could shape and forge as well as any cave-dwelling gnome. I made necklaces of silver droplets, gold armbands shaped like leafy vines, candlesticks, pitchers, ewers, and tongs. I went through a long goblet phase—fifty years at least. Eventually I moved on to weapons— but more of that later.

Finally, as I have said, I could recite each and every one of *The Rules Governing the Ladies of the Lake*, having committed the entire body to memory when I was ninety-eight. I was only a child then and eager to prove my cleverness, but my achievement (such as it was) proved to be of questionable value, for, having memorized the Rules, I was then bound to follow them—not only by honor, but also because the skin between my toes itched (sometimes quite painfully) if I did not.

This could be irksome.

Which brings me to Merlin.

Far too much has been said (and sung) about what passed between the great wizard and me, and almost all of it is irritating nonsense. I did not flirt with him, nor did I charm him into loving me. I did not crave his powers, and I most emphatically did not lock him up by turning his own magic against him. The truth—sordid and shocking enough to make me cringe for at least a hundred years—is far more interesting, and I fully intend to reveal it. Until then, I will say only this: Merlin did introduce me to Arthur, and in doing so changed my life forever.

❧

Merlin called on me one spring morning, just as the water lilies were opening to the sun. He did me the courtesy of coming into the Lake, but after I assured him that we could speak just as well on land, we floated to the shallows and then walked ashore. By this time the thrushes were singing, a lovely song, very liquid, about mayflies and grubs. We listened for a moment, and then Merlin told me why he had come.

"The future king of Britain will soon be needing a sword and scabbard," he said. "Will you fashion them?"

I said I would. As I mentioned, a Lady who can work metal is a rarity—like a sweet-voiced goblin or a fairy who likes numbers. But I enjoyed the gift and never questioned it. Perhaps—and this occurred to me many years later—I was given it so that I could perform this very task, which was more important than I knew.

In any event, even if I had wanted to refuse (and I did not), I was disallowed. *The Rule of Service to Future Kings* was clear about that.

"The sword must be invincible, and the scabbard must have the power to stanch his blood if he is wounded," Merlin continued.

Good idea for the scabbard, I thought, hoping I had the spell for it.

"Both should be heavily jeweled," he said, "as befits a king," and I nodded. I liked jewels. In fact, I loved them.

"And they must be ready in three years," he concluded.

"Impossible."

The wizard's long, thin nostrils flared, as if the word smelled bad.

"It will take me almost three years to forge and temper the blade," I told him, "and the grip alone requires a year. I will need nine years."

"Nine." He drew the word out, as if considering the number; at the same time the sky darkened and thunder rumbled directly overhead. "The boy is twelve," he said pointedly, "and will very soon be ready to take the throne." A bolt of lightning hit a tree on the horizon, and it toppled in flames.

Merlin, Merlin, Merlin! I thought. *Do you really think that roiling the weather will make me hurry? Think again!* I gave him a smile with just a hint of glamour in it (the girlish, honeylike sort). "Nine years," I repeated.

I was pleased to see his face soften. "Nine years it is," he said, as if there had never been a difference of opinion.

I nodded. The sky cleared. We touched palms and bowed, and I began to sink into the Lake.

"You won't forget the scabbard?" he called.

I shook my head. "Be sure to bring him when you return," I called back.

"Done," he promised, fading into the atmosphere.

CHAPTER 2

The underwater life is not for everyone, but that spring, after Merlin's visit, it suited me to perfection. I liked being on land well enough and the neighboring countryside was always richly beautiful, but no solid ground could offer the dreamy weightlessness and utter silence that my new task required, so in the Lake I stayed.

Knowing I would see the sword only if my mind was quiet, I gave myself over to the water. First I lay in the shallows with the lilies and reeds, listening to the insects. After nightfall I drifted out to the center, where the lavender moonlight was brightest. I turned over and lay facedown, arms outstretched.

Come to me, I thought.

And there, as the days passed, I waited for a vision. The

temperature of the water changed from warm to cool and back again. The sun chased the moon out of the sky and was chased by her in turn, and the Lake changed color every time—pink, blue, gold, scarlet, black, silver. Rain pocked the water's surface. Wind rippled it. Trout brushed my fingers, egrets sunned themselves on my back, a bullfrog used my head as a launching pad. No vision came.

Eventually I sank to the bottom of the Lake, where stubbly-skinned leviathan fish hovered in the dark. I hovered there with them, all volition gone. I do not know how much time went by, only that my mind grew very quiet. When it was hollow as an empty shell, I saw Excalibur.

Its golden pommel was set with a star ruby as big as a quail's egg. Its grip was dragon bone, bound with dragon hide. Its domed guard, studded with square emeralds and round sapphires, was incised with a pattern of crosses and circles. Its iron blade was seven hands high and gleamed majestically, as if housing a cold blue flame.

I felt a long thrill of delight—and then doubt set in. Could I make such a sword? In only nine years? That was hardly any time at all! Suddenly my smugness with Merlin seemed idiotic. *Drippy-faced ninny!* I thought, rising to the surface.

And now I saw that high summer had come. It was a season of blue skies and near-eternal days, when night came like an afterthought—shadows deepened, the light dimmed, but true darkness never fell.

Pleased that I would be traveling in daylight, I dressed in a gown of drab linen and veiled myself in homespun. I knew this humble costume—more suited to a supplicant than a Lady—might please the Lowly Gnomes, but never sway them. Still, I was bound to follow *The Rule of Thorough Preparation for a Difficult Task*.

Once ready, I set off for their domain.

CHAPTER 3

The Lowly Gnomes are reclusive. They are also wily, dishonest, and highly intelligent, traits that do not endear them to other spirits. Elves, trolls, and fairies dislike them; nixies and pixies fear them; and their cousins, the good-natured Nose-Rubbing Forest Gnomes, stay out of their way.

Dwarves, who pride themselves on their gruff candor, scorn the Lowlies and have feuded with them for centuries. The Lowlies, quicker-witted than the dwarves but smaller and weaker (they are knobby, amber-skinned, and ever so slightly hunched over, even the young ones), have never managed to prevail. This has made them bitter and more inclined to trade with folk such as myself for the magic they crave. Burning inside every Lowly breast was the painful notion that victory would be theirs if only they had the right magic—which was perpetually just out of reach.

I have never truly enjoyed my dealings with the Lowlies, fearing that they might unknowingly invoke a Rule that would thwart my purpose. It has never happened, but it could, and that would be disastrous. They are stubborn, tough negotiators, and even under normal circumstances, every bargain I have struck with them has cost me dear.

On the other hand, I have always left them knowing I have won something precious. Abhorrent as they are, the Lowlies trade in the largest, most luminous gemstones this side of the Narrow Sea, and right now, I needed them.

⚜

It was important to observe all the formalities, not only because *The Rule of Unwavering Politesse* demands it, but also because the Lowlies are quick to take offense, so as soon as a cluster of them appeared at the mouth of the cave, I bowed deeply. Then I gave their leader, Metite, the Fivefold Greeting, blessing his feet, knees, navel, heart, and brow. In typical Lowly fashion he protested, saying I should not trouble myself, but I saw by the inadvertent twitch of his crooked little mouth—not quite a smile, but close—that he was pleased. "The smaller the spirit, the greater the courtesy," as the saying goes.

Bent almost double, I followed Metite down a long, curving passageway whose gold-flecked walls gleamed dully in the torchlight. When we reached our destination, a tall, circular chamber with floors of immaculate white stone, Metite called for refreshments—tea smelling of mushrooms, pelletlike cakes resembling rabbit droppings—and watched attentively as I sampled them.

"Delicious," I lied. If we did not start trading soon, I might be pressed into eating an entire meal of Gnomish food, which was a dreadful prospect.

Fortunately, Metite did not dally. "It is a pleasure to see you, Damosel," he said in his surprisingly deep voice, "though your visit is unexpected. You are still happy with the moonstones, I hope?"

Many years before, I had bought a strand of moonstone beads from him and set them into a necklace for my cousin Nimue as a gift for her 120th birthday. Their soft radiance was so beguiling, and so perfect for a girl of her age, that I had bartered an excellent spell for them. Thus far I had not missed it—it was an unimportant helping spell that enabled a small creature to elude a large one, and then only briefly—but I have always regretted the exchange. It is not that I fear I will need the spell one day (*The Rule of That Which Has Just Been Lost* notwithstanding) but that I used magic frivolously.

The notion that magic should not be wasted is a recent one, gaining acceptance in the spirit world only three or four hundred years ago. Before then magic was abundant and taken for granted. My lucky forebears used it with abandon, casting spells as gaily as if they were tossing daisies. They never dreamed they were squandering it and had no idea of the consequences.

I, on the other hand, grew up knowing them all too well, for by my time there were three new Rules prohibiting the casual use of magic, and they were the first ones I learned. Only Avalon, the enchanted isle beyond the western horizon, was impervious to the threat; that remote, exclusive place, where only the best and worthiest spirits were admitted, would always be a place of abundant magic—or so I was taught. (And that is all I can reveal about my education.) The thought of a world without enchantment, the chill bleakness of it, always made me feel as if I were shriveling.

(I wish I could say the same for my fellow spirits. Far too many scorn the notion, blithely going on as before. If I were a different sort of Lady, I would curse them all.)

Metite's little black eyes never strayed from mine as he waited for an answer. "Very happy," I assured him, for Nimue adores the necklace and wears it always.

"Ah, good," he said. "And today you have come for . . . ?"

"Three emeralds, three sapphires, and a ruby."

"Precious gems," he noted with surprise, his gaze sharpening.

There was a brief silence as he gave me the opportunity to say more. Merlin had not enjoined me to secrecy, and telling Metite about the sword would do no harm, but I am naturally cautious, even secretive, so I steered the conversation into safer waters.

"Yes," I said noncommittally. "The emeralds must be square and the sapphires round. Also, the ruby must have a star in it."

"And the quality . . . ?" Before I could reply, Metite raised a hand. His spindly brown fingers ended in fingernails that curled over themselves, like talons. "I should not even ask," he said. "Damosel wants only the very best, is it not so?"

"Yes, Metite, you know me well," I replied with all the earnestness I could muster, and once again he was pleased.

"As I thought." He issued a Gnomish command to one of the attendants, who hurried away, returning a moment later with two silver caskets.

"You will be using the emeralds and sapphires in combination?" he asked, and when I nodded, the attendant placed the caskets side by side before me and opened them. At a signal from Metite, he tipped them forward and their contents spilled onto the floor.

I leaned forward, gaping like a bumpkin. There were two heaps of gems at my feet. The emeralds, all square, large as my pinkie nail and perfectly clear, were the cool, inviting green of moss in shade. The sapphires, a deep, shining purple-blue, were like rounded bits of the evening sky. It was a long time before I managed to tear my eyes away from them; when I did, I saw that Metite's face was impassive. How could he remain calm with such gems within reach? I had a very strong desire to scoop them up by the handful and run them through my fingers, but I quelled it. "I cannot choose from such an array," I said humbly (and truthfully). "It is beyond me. Will you help?"

Now he actually did smile. "Of course," he replied, and before I had selected a single emerald, he had taken three from the pile and was holding them out for my inspection. "These are the best, I think."

They beamed as brightly as if they had been plucked from a rainbow. "Perfect," I sighed. Another instant and I was admiring three equally dazzling sapphires.

"And now you will want to see a ruby?" he asked. At my nod he issued another command, and the attendant gnome disappeared, this time returning with a small golden casket. He knelt before me and opened it.

It is said that the Ladies of the Lake have dragon's blood, for they love gemstones as much as the great winged serpents do. I believe it, for at the sight of the ruby my blood stirred and warmed, my hands tingled, and my face grew hot. If I had had a tail, it would have twitched.

"Take it and hold it," urged Metite, "the better to see it shine."

I picked it up. It was deepest carmine, cool and smooth to the touch, with the pleasing weight of a quail's egg. And when I rolled it in my palm, the lustrous white star at its center flared brightly, as if yearning to emerge.

It is a stone that will take to spells, I thought. And because its receptivity to magic was even more important than its beauty, I resolved to have it.

Metite saw it in my face, of course.

"The price?" I asked.

"What will you offer, Damosel?"

I started off as modestly as I could. "One yearlong spell for the ruby, another for the three emeralds and three sapphires," I replied, "effective above- or belowground."

His spiky little eyebrows rose. "I think you can do better," he said, plucking the ruby out of my hand. I missed it immediately.

"Tell me what you would like," I said.

"An agelong spell for the ruby effective in three, not two, realms," he said. "One yearlong spell for each of the emeralds and each of the sapphires. All seven," he concluded, "with the power to help *or* hinder."

"That is a great deal of magic," I said. "More than I can give." His face became very still, and I wondered if I had angered him. Perhaps I would have to go elsewhere for the gems, which would be more trouble than I liked to calculate. On the other hand, I was one of the few beings who could, or would, offer Metite a taste of the power he craved; he might choose to overlook my bluntness. I hoped so.

"I will not give you a spell that works in water," I said. "Our Rules forbid it." This was true. "But I will give you three helping spells—one for the ruby, one for the emeralds, and one for the sapphires."

After a moment's silence, he replied, "The spell for the ruby must last an age."

"For a year. Like the others."

"Two years."

"One year and a half."

"Then it must be a two-sided spell, both helping and hindering."

Hindering spells are more powerful, and much more dangerous, than the helping kind. The strongest—the ones that can kill, or maim, or imprison an adversary for all time—are closely guarded. I knew only a handful and would never entrust one to Metite; he would put it to bad use at once and with glee.

Helping spells, on the other hand, are benign—tools, not weapons. So, heeding *The Rule Against Revealing Potentially Dangerous Information*, I countered, "Helping only."

Metite's response was to hold up the ruby so that its star caught the torchlight and beamed celestially. I managed to remain firm and repeated my offer. Having learned the hard way that Metite was impervious to glamour, all I could do was cross my fingers and wait. Meanwhile, he pursed his lips, examined each and every emerald and sapphire with dark solemnity, and then proceeded to fondle the ruby as if he were conversing with it. Just as I was beginning to lose hope, he raised his eyes to mine and said, "Done."

I gave him the spells, which he committed to memory as quickly as I spoke them. Then, after refusing his offer of further refreshment, I took the jewels and made a polite, if hasty, farewell.

I would really have to hurry now, I thought as I set out for home. I only had eight years, four months, and eleven days left.

CHAPTER 4

In early autumn I moved to my smithy, a cairnlike stone hut on a rock ledge overlooking the Lake and the sea beyond. Boasting three tiny windows and an ancient, dwarf-made anvil, its only furnishings were a driftwood table and a rough-hewn stool. There I set to work.

First I forged the blade, hammering the red-hot iron until it took shape. When its two sides tapered evenly and its tip curved just so, I annealed it, heating and cooling the metal until it was soft enough to grind. For this I used three stones—coarse, medium, and fine—going over and over the edges until they could cut through a feather on the wind.

(The blade passed its first test on a bright autumn day when the geese were flying south. The sky was a radiant blue, the wind brisk, the goose feather meeting the gleaming metal as if eager to divide—and so it did.)

That winter I hardened the blade, heating it, immersing it in brine, then quenching it in oil. I did this over and over until, in late spring, it passed its second test, cutting through a man-size, moss-covered stone as smoothly as a knife cuts cheese.

The very next day the dragon skin I had sent for finally arrived from Hibernia, so I put aside the blade and set to carving the grip. It may have been all the hammering and grinding I had been doing, but my hands were now so strong that the knife I used on the dragon bone felt like a plaything, and carving the hilt was as easy as peeling a carrot.

The dragon skin was another matter. It came from the gray-white underbelly (as I had specified), but even so, it was scaly and tough, so cutting it into long, even strips took great effort and even greater patience. By the time I had wrapped and glued the skin around the hilt, the geese had once again flown south and the air was chill.

As winter set in, I turned to making the guard and pommel. The gold I had set aside for them was so pure that it was soft in my palm, as malleable as clay. It yielded to the hammer with little urging, as if it had long known what form to take.

I finished the pommel in spring, soon after the feast of Beltane. In the world of mortals it was planting time. Here at home the wind had lost its bite and the first iris shoots were coming up around the Lake like spiky green fence posts. I finished the guard soon after, on a balmy day smelling of wild roses. As the bees droned in the flowers with busy satisfaction, I carried my table outside so I could work in the shade of the big oak tree and picked up my chisel.

From that moment on I enjoyed the pleasure that only

complete absorption brings, guiding my chisel in and out of the runes—circle, cross, circle, cross—until they formed an unbroken ring around the guard.

Then it was time to set the gemstones, a task I had been looking forward to ever since acquiring them, and not only because it would allow me to savor their hypnotic beauty. When the stones were in place and the sword assembled, I would put away my hand tools and work with magic instead.

❧

By fall, Excalibur's blade was burnished silver-white. Its guard gleamed with emeralds and sapphires, and the bright star in its pommel flickered restlessly. When the feast of Samhain came, I was ready to cast the first spell. Samhain Eve is the best night of the year for magic, a time when normal boundaries blur and firm convictions wobble. During those few hours, the right incantation can do great things.

So as darkness fell on the Eve, I cast the strongest helping spell I knew, calling on the runes to awaken Excalibur's power. The wind swept my chant into the sky, and when I raised the sword, black now against the rising orange moon, it juddered in my hands as if struck by lightning. Then it became so heavy that I had to set its tip on the ground.

Have it kill quickly, without causing pain, I thought. It was such an unusual quality for a sword that I wondered if it came from some long-forgotten Rule about the making of weapons.

I reminded myself that there were no Rules about the making of weapons.

Besides, the skin between my toes wasn't itching.

The notion of a merciful sword grew more and more appealing and I decided to put it to use.

The conjuring did not take long; then it was time to test the blade. I do not like to kill, and the prospect of dispatching anything with a sword, even one as fine as Excalibur, made me queasy. I put it off for most of a day, calling myself a silly fool. When I finally found the courage and the frog victim went peacefully, falling to the blade without a croak, I was happier than I like to admit.

Then I turned to enchanting the scabbard. I cast a spell that would keep Arthur from bleeding even a single drop, no matter how severe his wound. It was a powerful spell, ending in a deeply satisfying shout.

When my voice died away, I slipped Excalibur into its scabbard. The guard jewels flashed, and the runes, which had been quivering with a life of their own, finally settled into place.

I took a deep breath, feeling twin pangs of joy and sadness. Nine years had passed. Arthur's sword was ready for him.

He was tall, poling his raft with easy grace, a young man who looked nothing like a king. His tunic was as grimy as any foot soldier's, his boots were creased with heavy wear, and his face, weathered and ruddy, sported a good three days of ginger stubble. His hair was coarse and sun-streaked, swept back from his forehead. A wound, newly healed, hung above his right eye. He had been fighting hard.

"Arthur," I said, glimmering a little.

"Lady," he replied, with a quick, deferential nod, "I would ask a favor of you."

"And what is that?"

I had caused Excalibur to rise out of the water when Arthur and Merlin reached the Lake. A woman's pearly white hand held the sword aloft so that it shone in the morning sun. I did not have to read Arthur's mind to know that he was enraptured, and I could not blame him. It was a dazzling sight, produced, I might add, without extravagant magic.

"The sword in the Lake. Will you let me have it?" The direct request and the openness and warmth of his expression disarmed me. I had intended to exact a fee for the sword (there are many Rules concerning compensation to a Lady for her services, the first being *The Rule of Instantaneous Payment*), but now I wavered. Why not simply give it to him?

The impulse surprised me. It also made me wonder if the men who had joined Arthur at the very first, when his right to rule was so hotly disputed, had done so because he had inspired generosity in them also. It was a good quality in a leader, I thought, as long as he was trustworthy. Looking into his mind, I saw no guile, only resolution and purpose. I also saw a deep underlying sadness, but not its cause. Perhaps I would search for that another time.

I said, "The sword is called Excalibur, and you shall have it on two conditions."

"Whatever you wish, only tell me."

"First, when you no longer have any use for it, you must return it to the Lake."

"I will. And second?"

"You will grant me a favor when I request it."

"You have my word," he said, and again his head dipped almost shyly.

"Good. Take it, and use it as best you can," I said. "You should know," I added, "that it has the power to kill quickly and painlessly."

"Truly?" I saw that he was grateful.

"Yes." There are men who love to do battle, taking grim

pleasure, even joy, in destroying their enemies, and there are those who kill because it is their duty. For them the battlefield is unavoidable, a bloody passageway to some greater good. So it was with Arthur. "Make sure to take the scabbard also," I said.

He thanked me and rowed over to the sword, then grasped it and raised it above his head in a happy, triumphant gesture. For that brief moment he looked as young as he was. Still smiling, he rejoined Merlin, who had been waiting at the shore.

The mage and I exchanged glances across the water. His said, *You have done well*. Mine said, *So have you*.

CHAPTER 6

I am called Twixt now, and it is a fine name compared to Dungbeetle, which is what my first master called me. In those black years I often wished I was an insect. I would gladly have disappeared into a dung heap, but he would not allow that, oh no. He owned me, he had paid good money for me, and that gave him leave to dress me in bright colors and a cap with brass bells so that like a leper I could never pass unnoticed. But country folk did not shrink from me, as they did from lepers; I was not frightening, only ridiculous and small. Without seeming to, my master encouraged them to mock me, and while they did, he picked their pockets. It was not a happy life, nor a safe one. When he was finally caught and hanged in a village near Acqua Sulae, I feared I would die also, but that day the God of Luck (praise him!) answered my prayers. In the hubbub before my master's execution I escaped into the forest.

I'm free! I thought, so happy that the very tree bark seemed to sparkle.

But on the very next day Esus and his brother found me, and my troubles began anew.

I was in a thicket pulling blackberries off the branches when I heard them. Later on I kicked myself a dozen times for ignoring their hoofbeats. I could have found a better hiding place than the shrubbery. I could have run away. If I had, they would have kept lolloping by to spread their misery elsewhere.

But no, I was so hungry, so happy to be cramming a few berries into my mouth, that like a fool I ignored my ears even as the riders came close enough to see me dive into the bushes. Then it was too late.

Hunched down, I heard the horses blowing hard, smelled their pungent sweat. I covered my head with my arms. *Don't let them see me!* I prayed to the God of Luck, but he ignored me. A sword parted the branches above me and a loud voice said, "Here! What's this?"

His face was crisscrossed with scars and framed with black hog-bristle hair, his eyes bulging. Tufts of hair sprouted from his neck all the way up to his ears.

"You're not a bear!" he said. He poked the tip of his sword under my chin and forced my head up. The touch of cold metal made me want to scream.

"Ha! Told you!" the other man gloated. He rode closer, his blue eyes taking me in with too much interest. His pudgy face, short front teeth, and round, dimpled chin gave him the look of a baby possessed by evil spirits.

"A midgie!" he squealed. "They're good luck!"

I'm not good luck, I'm bad luck, I thought, *just ask my dead master!* But my throat was dry and my heart was beating like a tom-tom. I could no more speak than I could disappear.

"Good luck? We'll see about that," said the dark-haired man. "Come on, runt, out of your hidey-hole."

I straightened up. "My name's Twixt," I said.

"Your name is whatever we call you," said the baby-faced man. "Now listen to my brother or your ugly little head will roll."

I climbed out of the bushes, quaking. *I'm in for it now*, I thought, and I was.

❧

The big hairy one was Borvo and his baby-faced brother was Esus. I hated them both, but it was Esus I feared. Some people are good at music, or juggling, or picking pockets; Esus was good at spite. I was his favorite victim, for unlike his woman, Ofie, I was small and clawless and never with child.

Esus was cunning, too. I tried my best to stay out of his way, I hid in the storeroom, the horse shed, the chicken house, but he always found me. Even on the coldest days he came after me. It was a nasty game of hide-and-seek, and I was always It. When he found me out he'd grab me by my jerkin and haul me into the room where they took their meals. If I struggled, he'd shake me hard or wallop me. He was stronger than he looked, his round body hard-packed as a pig's.

Once inside, he'd go to Borvo, who most times was sitting at the hearth sharpening his knives. He had a lot of them.

"Brother," Esus would say, his manner sly and hateful, "should we make the runt earn his supper today?"

"Of course," Borvo always replied. Sometimes he was testing a blade or peering at a newly honed edge. The sure way he handled his knives made my guts wobble. "But how?" he would add, looking at me with narrowed eyes. If I tried to get away before Esus replied, it was never any good. Borvo would catch me or send his hounds to do it, which was worse, because their teeth were sharper.

Then it was just misery—either singing and dancing and doing cartwheels on the table while they got shouting drunk or being forced to drink with them until I passed out. I never let on that I knew how to juggle, they would have forced me to do it with Borvo's knives.

As it was, they often got me tipsy because it was so easy, less than a pint and I was teetering.

Once, in January, Esus forced me to stand against the big beech with a turnip on my head so Borvo could practice his knife-throwing. For days after I felt sick every time I passed the tree, seeing my outline on its trunk.

Another time, when I was so besotted that I could not even protest, they tossed me into the pond to see if I would drown. I would have, but Borvo pulled me out and kept whacking me until I vomited. I lay there shivering and choking until my mind cleared as if it had been wiped with a rag. I told myself I would get away if it killed me, and it almost did.

PART TWO

In Which Damosel Learns of Three Quests

CHAPTER 7

It was a long time before I saw Arthur again, but I did hear news of him, all good. Within a few years of our meeting he won over many of his foes. His prowess with Excalibur was celebrated, the mercy he showed his enemies much discussed. When he finally subdued the rebel kings of the north, he became a hero. His people, slow to accept him at first, now loved him.

During these early years, Merlin had used both cunning and magic to keep Arthur from harm. On the morning of a crucial battle between Arthur and the massed armies of King Lot and King Nero, Merlin visited Lot while he was arming himself in his tent, then distracted him with such fanciful stories that Lot actually forgot to join Nero on the field. With only one army to fight, Arthur won handily. And when Nero was killed in the rout, Lot lost his most important ally.

When he learned of the defeat (and understood how he had been duped), Lot's rage was monumental. He already hated Arthur; now he vowed to destroy him. Merlin was well aware of Lot's hunger for revenge, so he did his best to keep the two men apart. When Lot and Arthur finally made peace and four of Lot's sons came to court, Merlin never trusted them completely. Oaths of loyalty were one thing, blood oaths another, so he kept Gawaine, Gareth, Agrivaine, and Gaheris in his sights even after they were knighted.

But some things even Merlin could not change, and Arthur's fate was one of them.

The other was his own.

❦

I have already spoken of my cousin Nimue, a girl of eerie beauty and chill disposition. Males found her green eyes, her bee-stung mouth, and her languid grace irresistible, and when they pursued her, she toyed with them. Then, when they suffered (and they did, extravagantly), she watched them the way a child watches a caterpillar while poking it with a stick. Nimue didn't dislike men; she simply felt very little for them.

I confess that her mischief never troubled me overmuch. If she broke a few hearts here and there, what was the harm, as long as she broke no Rules? Besides, her swains were young and resilient, and they almost always recovered.

Further, Nimue was much bolder than I, and her droll, slightly malicious accounts of her adventures were always entertaining. So I was pleased when she came to visit shortly after Arthur's wedding. I had declined the invitation, knowing it would be a grand affair and far too crowded for my taste. I sent Nimue to Camelot in my stead. She, who had never suffered a moment of shyness in her life, was overjoyed.

By now the strange and magical occurrences marking this great event are well known. Merlin had a hand in them, but some say his hand slipped, that he lost control. I have often wondered if this was so, but in light of what befell him later, I never had the courage to ask. Still, by choice or by chance, Merlin's ensorcellation quickly became its own wayward creature, growing and expanding to encompass animals, knights, and ladies; curses and romance; a dwarf; a magic sword; three quests; and a beheading. Through it all the royal couple and their many guests were thrilled, frightened, and horrified.

In short, they all had a wonderful time.

Nobody but Merlin could have initiated such goings-on, and this was not lost on my little cousin. As she described the events to me (it was a fine summer afternoon, and we sat in dappled sunlight at the Lake's edge), Nimue's interest in the old wizard quickly became apparent. With her green eyes shining, she reported breathlessly that he had paid her this attention and that, uttered *deeply* wise things to her and her alone, and hinted strongly that he would like more of her company.

"*So* thrilling!" she purred, like a cat who had just bagged a sizable mouse. I agreed faintly, knowing that however she put it (or even chose to think of it), her interest in him was far from romantic. After all, Merlin was old enough to be her great-great-grandfather. It was his power that drew her.

I cannot say I was surprised. I had known for some time that Nimue was greedy for magic. Over the last few decades she had flirted with an elf (she lost interest when he told her that his only spells were for housework and shoemaking), a warlock ("Spells that produce loud, smoking dragon belches? No thank you!"), and a woodland mage called Ort, a large, good-natured denizen of the Forest Perilous. But Ort's skin was rough as bark, he shambled like a bear, and his best magic consisted of turning toadstools into salt. It was not much of a trick (though the deer loved him for it), but Nimue gave him no peace until he taught it to her. The moment he did, she left him. Needless to say, poor Ort was heartbroken.

Since then, Nimue had continued to hunt for spells, but the ones she managed to acquire were not much better than Ort's—"piffling," in her view. According to the Rules, this was as it should be: she was not meant to use serious magic until she became a full-fledged Lady, many decades hence. The restriction chafed, and she was openly impatient with it, as she was with any Rule that limited her powers. I had always been able to laugh at Nimue's wiles and caprices, but her avidity for magic was disturbing—unseemly, even coarse, given the shrinking supply. Moreover, we were kin, and it would reflect badly on me if she broke a Rule.

For all these reasons, I understood—and disliked—her fascination with Merlin. To my great shame, I never guessed where it would lead.

CHAPTER 8

"I never dreamed that he had such a flair for the dramatic!" she began. "From the moment he walked into the hall, he commanded *complete* attention. His flowing robes, his silvery beard, his dark, knowing eyes—he was the *picture* of wisdom! When he spoke, he hardly raised his voice, yet we all listened breathlessly, because of course he *sounded* wise, too! I was absolutely *weak* with delight to be seated next to him!

"Before he took his chair, he gazed around the crowded hall until all conversation stopped. Then he said, 'Take heed, for many wonders will be seen this day.' At his words (which were spoken with *deepest* gravity) Arthur and Guinevere froze, and such a hush fell over the entire company that we might have been at prayer. Everyone waited, scarcely breathing.

"No more than an instant passed," she continued, "and a white stag came bounding into the hall with a lovely white bratchet hot on its heels. She was followed by a pack of larger hounds, all brindled and slavering madly. There were already many dogs about, and they, too, joined the chase.

"The stag leaped over one table after another, knocking over the wine pitchers and trampling the food in the trenchers. The head of a roast boar took flight, apples and onions rolled, and more than one fine lady had her face spattered with currant sauce! As for the stag, just as it was preparing to leap again, the bratchet jumped up, bit into its flank, and would not let go. She was fierce for such a little dog.

"By this time the boar's head was on the floor and all the dogs in the hall were fighting for it. You cannot *imagine* the noise!" She was right: I could not.

"Meanwhile, the stag was rearing and flailing its hooves, trying to get free of the bratchet. Finally it succeeded. One of the guests, a knight, managed to catch it. And before any of us realized what he was doing, he ran out of the hall, mounted his horse, and rode away, taking the bratchet with him. The other hounds followed."

"And the stag?"

"It escaped."

I was glad to hear it. Stags are handsome animals.

"Scarcely a moment later," said Nimue, "a young woman rode into the hall on a handsome white palfrey, crying out that her bratchet had been stolen. 'Will you not help me, Sire?' she demanded of Arthur, for she had ridden up to the royal table before anybody could stop her. 'I must have my little dog back!'

"Her voice was harsher than a hoot owl's," said Nimue, "and her manner so overweening that Arthur, who (according to Merlin) is always kind to visitors, was startled into silence.

"When he failed to reply, she screeched so piercingly that a bird's nest fell out of the rafters. You would not have been able to stand it, Damosel!" said Nimue. She knew I disliked loud human noises.

"Fortunately, the lady was interrupted when a fully armed knight came galloping into the hall. Before she could resume her cries, he grabbed her horse's reins and pulled her away. When she was finally out of earshot, there was a mighty gust of relief.

"The king drained his wine goblet. 'By my soul, that woman was loud!' he exclaimed. 'I cannot say I am sorry that she is gone!' Many laughed at his vehemence.

"Meanwhile, Merlin leaned over to me with a mischievous smile. 'Watch what happens now!' he whispered. Then he stood, frowning deeply. He looked *very* fierce.

"I could not *imagine* what he was about to say or why he suddenly appeared so displeased!" she confided.

"And what did he say?"

"He said" (here she lowered her voice, imitating the wizard's somber delivery), " 'In dismissing that lady, my lord, you dishonor your wedding feast. Have you forgotten the royal tradition of honoring supplicants? It is a grave oversight and by no means a laughing matter.' "

I knew something of this tradition; it is like our *Rule of Heeding Heartfelt Entreaties,* which enjoins us to help the weak and powerless.

"Merlin's words captured everyone's attention," continued Nimue, "and I am sure that *nobody* suspected that he was only feigning anger—he was *most* convincing. Arthur, in particular, was suitably abashed.

"Then Merlin softened a little. 'Why not heed the law of the quest instead?' he suggested to the king, as if he had just thought of it. 'In that way you may still help the lady recover her dog. Send your knights out.'

"Arthur seemed glad for the solution. 'Why not, indeed?' he exclaimed. 'Done! Let's have a quest!'

"This caused a commotion of shouts and table pounding. When it died down, Merlin said, 'Three quests might be better, my lord.'

" 'Name them,' Arthur replied.

"Merlin looked out over the assembly. He pointed to a young knight—dark-haired and *very* handsome—sitting near the king's table. 'Sir Gawaine,' he called, 'you shall bring us the stag.' Gawaine stood with the air of someone who was often singled out, appearing not *the least bit* surprised. He is the king's nephew," she added, "so I suppose he is accustomed to favor."

Undoubtedly, I thought. Gawaine's mother, Margause, was Arthur's half sister; his father, King Lot.

"Sir Tor, on the other hand, was astonished when Merlin called on him," said Nimue. "When he leaped up—and it was quite a spectacle, for he is extremely tall and thin as a stick—he was positively *beaming*. His quest, said Merlin, would be to find the lady's white bratchet.

"The third knight was Sir Pellinore," said Nimue, "and he looked just as surprised as Tor when Merlin chose him. He is a seasoned knight of some age, long past the need to prove himself. Still, charged to find the lady who lost her bratchet and the knight who abducted her, he seemed just as pleased as the others.

"The three men—Gawaine, Tor, and grizzled Pellinore—knelt before the king, who wished them good hunting.

"Then, amidst much excitement, they departed."

CHAPTER 9

The day was growing warm, so Nimue and I moved closer to the Lake, where we could sit with our legs in the water. Then she resumed her account.

"I will start with Sir Gawaine," she said, splashing her feet. "You know he is the eldest son of Arthur's half sister Margause?"

I nodded. Margause and her husband, King Lot of Orkney (the same King Lot Merlin had tricked years ago, before a battle with Arthur), had five sons. Gawaine, Gaheris, Gareth, and Agrivaine were already at Camelot. The fifth, Mordred, was not quite old enough yet.

"Gawaine and his brother Gaheris—the next oldest, but nowhere *near* as handsome—rode off at once with their hounds in search of the stag. It was a fine day for a hunt, cool and bright, and for some time they rode along in silence."

"You followed them?" I asked.

"I was curious," she said quickly. "And Merlin told me I might enjoy trailing them unseen." *And perhaps your interest in him was shifting to young Gawaine,* I thought hopefully—and wrongly, as it turned out.

"At any rate," she went on, "it was very quiet after the hub-bub of the wedding feast—until, that is, the hounds suddenly gave cry and took off. The brothers galloped after them, and when they caught up with the pack, Gaheris cried out, 'There it is!' pointing straight ahead. Far in the distance was the object of their quest, the stag, looking pale and insubstantial as a ghost.

"The stag saw them, raced away, and disappeared from sight. And from then on, no matter how hard they pushed their horses, the brothers could not get closer to it. Instead it sprang into view and then disappeared, over and over again, like an apparition.

"When Gawaine and Gaheris emerged from the forest, they could see the stag running toward a castle atop a steep hill, with the hounds in hot pursuit. They followed, galloping across field after field and then through a marsh *teeming* with herons. The birds were not at all pleased—they flapped and cawed as the party thundered through, and their outcry con-tinued until riders and hounds were halfway up the hill.

"Finding the castle gates open, the brothers rode into the courtyard. Paying no heed to the two horses tied there—though they were jigging and pulling uneasily—they dis-mounted and hurried into the castle.

"And there they were met by a *most* woeful sight," said Nimue. "Gawaine's overeager dogs had felled the stag and it lay bleeding on the floor. The lord of the castle, a big man with thinning hair, having stabbed two of the dogs with his dagger, now dropped the weapon with a curse. Ignoring the brothers—who had just appeared—he knelt beside the dying stag.

"Taking its head in his arms and stroking it, he lamented, 'My beauty! My own dear one! What have they done to you?'"

"How terrible!" I said.

"I was so distressed that I almost became apparent," confessed Nimue. "But I caught myself in time, and I didn't. I didn't leave then, either, which was a mistake."

"Why?" I asked, wondering how the story could get any worse.

She leaned over to take a sip of Lake water and continued.

"Gawaine was in a chill fury. 'Why did you attack my hounds?' he demanded. 'They were only doing as they were bid! You should have struck at me instead.'

"'They murdered my pet, my wife's gift to me,' replied the lord, glaring back at him. 'That is reason enough.' He got to his feet; standing, he *loomed* over Gawaine. 'Remain if you dare,' he said. 'If you are here when I return, I will send you straight to hell, after your dogs.'

"'You can try,' retorted Gawaine, but the lord had already gone. A moment later he was back, wielding sword and shield. He advanced on Gawaine, then lunged at him swiftly. Gawaine fended him off, but the bigger man pressed on, forcing Gawaine back toward the wall, where he could be pinned and finished. The man's size and skill were *so* much greater than Gawaine's that Gaheris looked openly fearful for his brother.

"Then Gawaine's youth began to help him. He had been struggling to hold his own, but now he was nimble enough to elude one blow, and then another and another, until he was clear of the wall. At the same time the lord's breath grew ragged and his face ashy. Perhaps he was ill," commented Nimue, shrugging, "or older than he appeared, but when Gawaine saw him weaken, he seized the offensive. He must have thought that if he persisted, he could harry the lord to exhaustion, so that is what he did. As he was young and vigorous, it took very little time, and soon the lord was on his knees, gasping for mercy.

"'I have none for you,' said Gawaine with cold finality. 'You killed my hounds.' As Gaheris looked on, he forced the man to lie flat on the floor and raised his sword high. At that moment the lady of the castle ran into the hall, crying out for Gawaine to stop. But he could not—his sword was already coming down with *terrible* force, so that when the lady stumbled and fell across her husband's body, the blade struck *her*, not her husband, and she was beheaded."

CHAPTER 10

"No!" I was aghast.

"There is more," said Nimue, her green eyes bright. "Gaheris stared in disbelief at the lady's body, and when he could speak—for at first he could not—he said hoarsely, 'For *shame*, Gawaine! Where is your heart? You cannot be a knight if you have no mercy!'

"Gawaine stood there, eyes lowered. If he felt remorse, he gave no sign, but only breathed out hard, as if he had been struck in the chest with a pike. At length he muttered to the noble, 'Arise. I will spare you.'

"'What good is your mercy now?' shouted the man, his face livid with his wife's spattered blood. 'You have killed everything that is dear to me!'

"'I am sorry,' said Gawaine. 'I did not mean to.'

"The lord sobbed, 'I wish I were dead.'

"'What is your name?' asked Gawaine.

"'Ablamar of the Marsh.'

"Gawaine helped him to his feet. 'Go to King Arthur,' he said, 'and tell him you were overcome by the knight in quest of the white stag.'

"When Ablamar hesitated, Gawaine said, 'Go before my pity runs out.'

"'Your pity!' Ablamar spat the words, his big hands trembling at his sides. Gawaine did not reply—instead he brought in one of the horses from the courtyard and draped the dead stag's body over the back of its saddle. 'Show the stag to the king,' he said."

"Proof of his quest?" I ventured, and my cousin nodded.

"Once again he told Ablamar to go, and this time the man said nothing, but only climbed onto his horse and rode away.

"Then," said Nimue, "Gawaine behaved *most* strangely. Instead of leaving the castle, he sauntered through the hall, passing the headless body of Sir Ablamar's wife without a glance. Gaheris followed, first bewildered, then aghast, as his brother found a sleeping chamber, laid his sword on the bed, and removed his bloodstained boots.

"'Why are you disarming?' he demanded. 'We must leave at once! This castle is not safe for either of us.'

"'For the moment it is ours,' Gawaine replied. 'And I am weary. Surely we can rest here for a while.'

"'No!' protested Gaheris. As if to prove his point, four knights charged into the chamber shouting that Gawaine had dishonored his knighthood by denying mercy to their lord and that he, Gawaine, deserved none himself. He would soon experience such agonies that he would welcome death, they said. One of them left to find tongs and pincers, another to fetch chains.

"Next," said Nimue, "one of the remaining knights shot Gawaine in the arm with an arrow, which was quite a feat because the chamber was *very* small. Ignoring his wound, Gawaine told Ablamar's men that they had no authority over him, and no right to judge him either, because he was a prince. His arrogance so inflamed the knights that they swore to run him through right then and there. And they might have," said Nimue, "if four ladies of the castle had not flown into the chamber at that very moment.

"Now there was barely room to *sneeze*, much less wield a sword," she said, "so the ladies persuaded the knights to leave. Then they bound Gawaine's wound, assuring the brothers all the while that the castle dungeon was a goodly size, almost as big as the very chamber they were in, and that Gawaine and Gaheris would find it tolerably comfortable, as soon as they stopped minding the dark and the wet. With this they departed, locking the door behind them.

"When they were at last alone, Gaheris observed gloomily that the questing life was not for him.

"'What do you mean?' Gawaine demanded testily.

"'Look at us!' replied Gaheris, with equally bad humor. 'One day out on our first adventure and we are prisoners! If we ever get back to Camelot,' he declared, 'I will not stay. I will find some other livelihood.'

"'Blateration!' snorted Gawaine.

"'I mean it,' insisted Gaheris. 'I would rather take up embroidery than make an ass of myself like this!'

"Gawaine conceded that knighthood was a parlous state. 'But there must be glory in it somewhere,' he insisted.

"Gaheris told him he was a glimmerless idiot. They bickered on and on," said Nimue, "until I grew so impatient that I left them and returned to Camelot."

"Were they killed?" I asked, noting that Nimue's appreciation of Gawaine's good looks had not moved her to help him. But I was not surprised. As I have said, she is somewhat heartless.

"Patience!" she chided, which was a fine example of the crow calling the raven black, in my opinion. Then she said, "No, they weren't killed. They arrived at court the next morning. The king was pleased to see Gawaine—until he got a good look at him, that is. Then his welcoming smile faded, and he stared at the knight in frank dismay.

"Gawaine was *truly* a gruesome sight," continued Nimue, "for entwined around his neck was a mass of yellow hair, and hanging from it was the severed head of the lady of the castle."

"No!" I felt slightly ill.

"Oh yes. And you cannot *imagine* the effect it produced. Guinevere teetered in her chair, as if she might faint (though she did not), and for a moment the king said nothing. Then he inquired—very evenly, as if holding himself *rigidly* in check, and so icily that the very *air* seemed to grow cold—'What is the meaning of this, Gawaine?'

"Gawaine recounted his adventure without emotion," said Nimue. "He did not falter once, even when he came to the moment when he accidentally killed the lady."

"And the lady's . . . ?" I could not even say the word.

"Head?" asked Nimue. I nodded. "It seems that when his captors learned that Gawaine was the king's nephew, they freed him—but not until he swore to wear the lady's head until he confessed his crime to the entire court.

"When he finished," she went on, "the silence in the hall was *profound*.

"At last Arthur spoke. 'Your youth, your inexperience,' he said, 'neither can excuse such cruelty, Gawaine. If you wish to serve me, you must renounce your low impulses. There is no place here for vengeful acts, or spite, or mean behavior. Do you understand?'

"Gawaine dropped his eyes, breathing hard. At that moment he looked naked and exposed, no longer the arrogant young royal. 'Yes, my lord, I understand,' he replied hoarsely.

"Until this moment Guinevere had not said a word. Indeed," commented Nimue, "throughout the festivities she had seemed content to play the young, wellborn bride, smiling prettily and saying little. But now she spoke up, her voice high and clear.

"'Take an oath before us, Sir Gawaine,' she said. 'Swear that from this day on, you will defend all women in distress. Swear also that you will never again deny mercy to any living soul.'

"Gawaine swore, and at *last* he was unburdened of the lady's head. This done, he bowed and left the hall. I could not swear to it," added Nimue, "but think I saw tears in his eyes."

"Of shame?" I wondered.

She raised an eyebrow. "Anger, more likely."

CHAPTER 11

All winter long I thought of nothing but escape, and soon my brain ached with the thinking, for it seemed fruitless, a bitter joke with myself the butt. I had suffered much in my life, blows and curses and deviltry, yet nothing before had ever brought me so low. Voices in my noggin told me I was stupid and useless, and every day I stayed with those cursed brothers, I believed the voices more. No longer did I think I was clever, simply playing the fool to keep alive. I *was* a fool, and I hated myself for it.

Then spring came and the two of them were jousting again. In the cold months they stayed at home and drank, they were like cave-bound bears, but when the weather turned they remembered the joys of killing and plunder. They forced me to stop any knight who happened by and say he could not pass unless he fought. It was a task I hated for I knew the outcome, it was an ugly one.

The brothers would kill and strip the knights of their belongings, as much for the pleasure as the gain. They never fought fairly. If it needed both of them to fell a man (for there were knights who could defeat a single brother, and some came close), all the better—foul play was the very froth on their ale. I yearned to warn the knights, but Borvo said if I tried he would cut me up and throw me to the pigs, and I believed him.

Every time the brothers fought I prayed they would die, and when they did not, the disappointment sickened me. The God of Luck was keeping his distance, so I began to pray for magic, for a wizard or a fairy to stop Esus and Borvo with a binding spell, a very painful one. And if the magic brought a few coins and a new suit of clothes for me, so much the better.

Weeks passed and I wished in vain. Then Sir Tor appeared.

I will never forget the day, it was Midsummer's, the longest of the year. There had been little traffic through the forest of late, and with nobody to fight, Esus and Borvo were restless, their filthy tempers worsening by leaps and bounds. It was only a matter of time before they turned on me, so when a young knight appeared that morning, I could not help but feel relief.

I hurtled toward him from my hollow tree waving my tin horn and shouting, "Stop!" and he laughed, showing two snaggly teeth. He was very tall and thin, at first glance ungainly. His clothes were patched, his horse and arms the poorest sort. Everything about him was shabby save his manner.

"What is your name, sir?" he asked. Nobody had ever called me "sir" before, and I was flummoxed. "T-Twixt," I stammered.

"I am Sir Tor," he said, "on quest for King Arthur." With this he wished me good day and made as if to spur his horse.

I raised my hand. "You cannot pass unless you joust with my masters. They will not have it otherwise."

He considered my words. "How many are they?" he asked.

"Two," I said. "Brothers."

"Well, then, summon them."

I blew my horn and when Esus and Borvo appeared, something moved me to warn the knight. I had never dared such a thing before, and my voice nearly failed me, but I whispered quickly, "Be wary, sir! They will do anything to win. And they always kill." He gave no sign of hearing me, yet I was sure he did. He might be poor and gangly but he was no coward, that was plain to see.

I always left before the combat, I had no stomach for it. To me these fights between the brothers and some hapless knight were sad events. But this time a tiny painful twinge of hope made me stay. I scrambled into my hollow tree. I would watch from there, praying for Tor to smite the brothers down as they deserved.

They galloped into the clearing on their big mounts, armed with swords, daggers, and shields. When they took Tor's measure it was clear what they thought. A young knight so poorly armed was easy pickings.

"I will take him," said Esus, advancing a little and drawing his sword. "You there," he called to Tor, "are you ready?"

"I am."

Esus hawked and spat, then charged with his weapon outstretched. Tor blocked him smoothly, scarcely raising his shield, then struck back hard, catching Esus just above the ear with the flat of his sword. It was a heavy, well-placed blow and Esus came tumbling down. He hit the ground face-first and lay there like a dead man, a sight that truly warmed my heart. Then he staggered to his feet and ran unsteadily at Tor, who had turned his horse and was approaching. Before he reached Esus he began to dismount. It was one of the rules of fighting, I knew from listening to Esus and Borvo, when one man came down, his opponent should also dismount to fight on foot. But the brothers derided the rules and never followed them. Tor was not even out of his stirrups when Esus slashed at his old horse's chest and the beast fell shrieking.

Tor's face turned gray. "What!" he shouted, jumping down. "You cut my horse?" Esus did not reply, he lunged at Tor instead. But his low maneuver gained him no advantage. Tor parried nimbly, then struck Esus's right arm with force enough to make it bleed. He moved so gracefully he could have been dancing. As awkward as he first appeared, he was a very good fighter, he made it look easy. Groaning, Esus swayed and dropped his sword, then fumbled for his dagger, but he was far too slow. Tor stopped him at swordpoint.

"Yield," he said.

"I will not!" Esus raised his voice, a signal for help. Borvo came forth quickly with his weapon drawn. "Leave him," he said to Tor.

"Stay back, sir, or you will be next," snapped Tor.

"I *am* next, you bloody ass," answered Borvo, kicking his great black horse.

And now Sir Tor was facing two opponents. He was not bothered, he stood there eyeing one, then the other as if choosing apples at a fruit stall, not defending his life. I was near pissing myself, yet could not tear my eyes away.

Esus ran at Tor waving his dagger, but before he could use it Tor hit him with his shield and caught him on the jaw. The shield was old, but its sharp metal studs did their work. Esus fell back making choking noises, then dropped and lay still. I knew he would stay there dead or no, the fat baby-faced coward.

That left Borvo. He charged at Sir Tor and swiped at him with his sword. A slower man would have found himself wondering where his head had rolled, but Sir Tor was quick and smooth, too, he evaded the stroke as easy as shrugging.

"Dismount, sir," he said as Borvo wheeled around. Borvo ignored him. He spurred his horse hard and rode at Tor again.

I feared that Borvo had the upper hand because he was mounted, but I was wrong. His big horse was strong and fast, but being a horse he did not like surprises, and now he got one. Instead of standing his ground as he had done before, Sir Tor ran at him brandishing his shield and shouting, "Back! Back!" It was quite a sight. The beast's eyes rolled, he bucked and reared, throwing Borvo, then galloped away. Borvo fell heavily. Like it or not, he was now truly dismounted, lying there with one leg twisted under him and the other twitching. He opened his eyes to find Tor's sword an inch from his face.

"Yield," said Tor. Borvo's heavy dark face purpled. He snarled a curse I will not repeat, a reference to Tor's mother. Tor whacked him on the nose. It must have hurt. I heard a crunch.

"Yield," he repeated. There was no mistaking the warning

in his voice, even Borvo took note. Besides, his leg was out of joint. He could not rise.

"I yield," he muttered. My heart soared. It was a dream come true.

All this time Esus had not moved. He lay where he had fallen, his eyes shut. His horse had bolted into the forest after Borvo's but now came ambling back with grass in his mouth and his reins dragging.

I left my tree. "Take the horse, Sir Tor," I said. "Their arms, too."

He was startled to see me but not displeased. "Hullo, Twixt!" he said amiably.

I wanted him to have his just rewards. "They're yours," I said. "You won them fairly." I looked down at Borvo, and for once I did not hide my contempt.

His face went purple with rage. "Shut up, you little maggot!" he shouted. "Get back to the house!"

Never, I thought. I looked up at Tor. "You've won me, too," I said. "Let me serve you." *Please please please*, I thought. *I will do anything.*

"Shut up!" screamed Borvo, thrashing on the ground. He kicked out hard at me with his good leg, but I hopped out of reach. *You and your knives!* I thought. *You missed your chance to kill me, and now it's too late.* He screamed again as if he had heard me.

"How old are you?" asked Sir Tor.

"Seventeen, I think."

He smiled. "Well, I have a year on you, I am eighteen, so you must do as I say."

"I will," I promised.

We tended to his horse first. I held its head while Tor studied its wound. The cut was long but not deep, and Tor was much relieved. "You'll live, old boy," he said, giving it a pat, then coaxing it to its feet.

"You will ride him and I will take the black," he said. "Can you do that?"

I quailed. A horse's back was much too far from the ground, not at all where I wanted to be. But at that moment I would have jumped on a hornet's nest for Tor. "Yes," I lied.

"Good," he said. "Help me." I did as he asked, collecting the weapons, packing up, all the while ignoring Borvo's bitter curses. Then Tor lifted me and I was in the saddle, clutching the reins and a hank of mane, too.

I had often rehearsed my farewell to the brothers, a short blunt speech comparing them to vermin and wishing them endless torment in the afterlife. But when it came to my actual leave-taking, they were spared. Intent on riding my new master's horse, I did not think of them at all.

Chapter 12

The day was warm, and we langered along at the only pace for me, a slow one. When we stopped at a stream so the horses could drink, I asked Tor about his quest. He told me it was for a white bratchet. Why would a knight risk his life for a dog? I asked, and he said it was the king's command, it must be obeyed.

An odd command, I thought, but then I knew nothing of kings, much less proper knights. I had only been with scoundrelly ones. Tor was kind and full of purpose, as different from Esus and Borvo as a pasty from mud pies.

As we crossed the stream, he said he had heard there was a small hunting party encamped nearby. "A farmer's boy told me it was near a priory."

"And they know of the bratchet?"

"Mayhap," said Tor.

"The priory is west of here." I did not know how far, for I had never been there. That was to change, and all too soon.

"Then we're off," said Tor. "Ready?" he asked.

"Yes," I lied. He turned his horse and made a quiet clicking sound. The horse broke into a run. Then we were galloping— through thickets and clearings, up hill and down, the ground beneath us a green blur looking far softer than it was, I knew this for a fact. I clung to my horse like a tick on a heifer, when he jumped a log or a rivulet I closed my eyes and moaned. There was no miscomfort too harsh, no price I would not pay to be free of those evil brothers, but when we finally came to the priory I was more than happy, and my poor bottom was happier still.

There was singing coming from the priory church, voices rising and falling, sweetly intertwined. Beyond the buildings was a shady little dell, grassed and bounded by a freshet. Two pavilions sat there, one white and one red, both with their curtains down. Nothing stirred but the rushing water. I looked to Tor for instruction.

"Wait here," he said, dismounting and giving me his reins. "Don't run away."

"I would never—" I began, then saw that he jested. "I will plant myself here like a tree," I vowed solemnly. That made him smile.

He walked into the red pavilion. I heard yelping, and out he came carrying a white hound.

"Take her," he said. My stomach fell. Dogs have never liked me, I have the tooth marks to prove it. I took the hound gingerly. It wriggled and whined in my arms, its black eyes with their white lashes fixed on mine as if waiting for a sign. "Hello," I said, and it licked my face. I sputtered. It kept licking.

Tor took his reins. "She likes you," he said, mounting his horse and spurring it on.

A young woman, her hair undone, ran out of the red pavilion. "What are you doing?" she cried. "Give the dog back to me!"

"I cannot," said Tor. "She is my quest and goes to the king at Camelot."

"No!" she shrieked.

Tor shook his head regretfully. "Yes," he said.

"You will pay dearly! My lord will have your head in a basket!"

We went on our way. "You would think the dog was made of gold, with all this hue and cry," said Tor.

"Perhaps she does tricks," I ventured. I had once seen a dog, a tiny little thing with a stubby tail, run up and down a teeter-totter.

"Perhaps," said Tor without conviction. Then he told me about the wedding feast, how the dog ran into the hall chasing a white stag and was carried off by a knight. "No sooner had they gone," he said, "than a young woman on a palfrey appeared, crying to the king that she must have her precious dog back at once."

"That woman?" I asked, meaning the one we had just left.

"Another one," he said, "though no less . . . forthright."

I wondered if *forthright* meant "wails like a banshee."

"Before the king could tell her yea or nay, a knight rode in, took hold of the woman's bridle, and made off with her."

It was all a jumble to me except for the white bratchet, who was draped across my horse's withers. I dared to pat her once and her tail flopped lazily. I did it again. Her back was sleek and warm. Losing her might well be cause for dole, I thought.

"It was after she was taken," Sir Tor went on, "that the king and Merlin sent us on quest—Sir Gawaine for the white stag, myself for the bratchet, and Sir Pellinore for the lady and the knight who abducted her."

"And now is your quest complete?"

"We shall see." He smiled so that his snaggleteeth showed.

I will not say the riding was easy for me, it was not, but as the hours went by I lost some of my fear. Meanwhile, the forest spoke in its quiet afternoon voice, bird trills and brief scurryings and the occasional buzz of an insect. Then the bratchet's ears went up, she whined, and we heard another sound, a horse coming our way. Tor's hand went to his sword.

A young rider, well armed, came out of the trees. He stared at me, astonished. I was used to stares and did not like them, but being on a horse took some of the sting out of his stupid gaping. *Now there's a surprise*, I thought, sitting up straighter and staring right back at him.

"Give me the bratchet," said the young man to Tor by way of greeting. Her tail twitched and she growled. I patted her.

"No," said Tor, "I am taking her back to Camelot."

"You will have to fight me first."

They rode at each other. With the clash of meeting they both came off their horses, then recovered quickly, circling with swords upraised. This knight was nothing like those spit gobbets Esus and Borvo, still, I did not like his looks. I hoped Tor would trounce him and quickly.

But they were too evenly matched for that. Tor blocked the

man's blows one after the other but could not manage to land one. They ran at each other again and again, their swords clanging and whining. It seemed they would never tire.

Meantime the sun disappeared. The wind came up and thunder rumbled, a deep deep sound like the sky's vexation. The bratchet shook, then burrowed into my armpit, and at that instant Tor caught the man on the shoulder, cutting him so he bled. The man struck back, but too slowly. Tor's next blow brought him down. He fell against the bole of a lightning-splintered tree.

"Yield," Tor said conversationally.

The other man pulled himself upright, breathing hard. "Not until I have the bratchet," he replied.

It started to rain.

The air grew chill. The rain slapped at us, the ground turned to muck. I shivered. If this was questing, I could live without it. *Oh, give up*, I told the man silently, wishing he would obey.

"Yield," Tor repeated. The man tried to stand but his legs gave out and he plopped down into the mud. He cursed the bratchet roundly, then hoisted himself up until he was on his feet. Clutching his wounded shoulder with mucky hands, he muttered, "No dog is worth this."

I could have told you that, I thought.

Tor waited.

"Enough, I yield," said the man disgustedly. Tor helped him onto his horse and he rode into the forest without a backward glance. When he was well away, Tor smiled, merry as a cricket. "*Now* my quest is over," he said.

At nightfall a hermit took us in. He was a rheumy old soul

with failing eyes, he thought I was Tor's little son. We slept on his floor, the bratchet curled up against me as cozy as you please. Next morning the hermit fed us and blessed us. When he patted my head in farewell saying, "Good lad," I did not mind a bit.

CHAPTER 13

We rode all morning. I was hurting in places I never knew I had, but Tor assured me I was getting the knack, I would feel better in no time. He was in a fine mood and so was the bratchet. She ran alongside us with her tongue lolling out, smiling.

Every time I thought of Esus and Borvo and how the distance between us was growing, I smiled, too. In fact, I was well content until I saw the castle. Camelot's walls were great and broad, the towers tall beyond my ken and crowned with gold to boot. The long road we traveled was teeming now with people carrying sacks and baskets, driving donkeys, riding bullock carts piled high with goods. All were going our way. A great many folk milled about the stalls outside the castle gates, buying and selling and passing the time. I had never seen such crowds, not even in the market towns where I had played the japer. The throngs cowed me. So did the castle. But it was thinking about what would happen when we reached the castle that frightened me most.

Tor had freed me from Esus and Borvo, he had given me work at my request. All the while he had treated me like a person, not a clod of dirt. Now we were at Camelot and he would have no further use for me. I was too small to be a proper squire. I could barely hold the horses, much less saddle them. All I had was my willingness, and surely that was not enough. He would let me go.

Meanwhile, he was humming a tune, whistling a few notes every now and then. He was happy and so was the bratchet. Only I was full of dread.

When we were a stone's throw from the gates, Tor hung back until we were abreast. "Now, Twixt," he said, "are you ready to meet your king?" It was a simple question, posed so affably that for a moment I forgot my misgivings. *What could be easier than entering a castle as big as a mountain and meeting the leader of the realm and his new queen? Tor says Arthur is a fine king. He might accept me.*

More likely not, snapped the part of me with a working brain.

"I suppose so," I answered.

"Then . . ." He took a breath and spoke with care. "You know the way people are, the way they take objection to what is not familiar? Or mock it?"

I nodded. I knew nothing better, it was the story of my life.

"When I bring you into the Great Hall there is bound to be a stir, perhaps some laughter, but you must ignore it. You helped me greatly, and I will say so. I will tell the king I could not have finished my quest without you."

I was too surprised to speak. This was not what I expected. Then Tor asked, "Do you know how to bow?"

I nodded again. My first master taught me.

"Good," he said as we rode through the gates. "You'll be doing a lot of it today." In the forecourt two stable boys greeted him with broad smiles. One, called Severn, took his reins. The other, not much bigger than me, took his shield. They were well mannered. When Tor helped me down, they did not gape or snicker once.

Tor raised his eyebrows as if to ask was I ready. *How could I be ready for this?* I thought, but here came another lie: I nodded yes.

With that he strode into the hall, and like a good squire I followed.

CHAPTER 14

It was just as Tor said about the stir. A great hum rose up at our appearance, the sound pocked here and there with laughter. The place was of a vastness, the light streaming down from windows up high colored like a rainbow. Smelling the spices, the food, the people, feeling the press of so many eyes on me, I thought, *It is like entering a village, a very rich one.*

I followed Tor down the center aisle between rows of tables, the guests jostling to see us. There must have been hundreds. Beyond Tor was a clear space and after that a platform and the royal table. *Arthur!* I thought, scarcely believing I was in his presence.

Tor had told me to keep my eyes down, but I could not help stealing a glimpse of the king. According to Tor, they were much the same age, but the king's face said otherwise, being weathered and lined. He was handsome nonetheless, with ginger hair, steady dark eyes, and an open expression. *Generous*, I thought. Seeing him, my hands unclenched and my throat loosened. I could swallow again.

Then we were before him.

I bowed along with Tor, the bratchet sitting at my side as pretty as you please.

"Welcome, Sir Tor," said the king. "Have you fulfilled your quest?"

"Yes, Your Majesty," said Tor. "Here is the proof." He patted the bratchet's head and her tail swished on the stone floor. There was a wave of laughter.

"Indeed," said the king. "And your companion? Is he proof of something also?" All eyes were on me now, including Tor's. His reply came quickly.

"Only that help can come in unexpected ways." He waited for the laughter to die down and said, "This is Twixt, my lord. He cautioned me against my first opponents, saying they were treacherous, and so they were. His warning helped me greatly." Tor inclined his head toward me, but I needed no prompting. I stepped forward and gave the king my handsomest, deepest bow.

"Well done, Twixt," said the king. His words were like a gift, my ears warmed with pleasure. Then Tor described his quest, making much of what I did. There were many approving murmurs. The queen smiled at me. By the time he finished I was standing tall, my whole self a-tingle, even my scalp.

The king said Tor had done exceedingly well for a new-made knight with only the poorest accoutrements. The stern old man on the king's left inclined his head in agreement while I puzzled over the word *accoutrement*. Perhaps it was a weapon or a horse.

"I will add my praises to the king's," said the old man, rising from his seat. A beautiful young girl sat beside him. She wore a necklace of round stones, each one shining like a moon. Her black hair was dressed with pearls. They shone, too. As he spoke, her green eyes never left his face.

"And I will offer a prediction," he said. With this the hall fell silent, the king and queen, the guests, the very birds in the rafters listening hard.

"Sir Tor, your future deeds will make the ones you have described today seem paltry. You will be one of the king's best, most courageous knights and remain always in his favor."

Tor's cheeks reddened. He cleared his throat. "Thank you for your kind words, Merlin," he said.

The king smiled. "As one familiar with Merlin's prophecies, I can tell you that kindness has nothing to do with them."

He said it very dryly, but the old man's eyes flashed, he seemed flattered. A look of great affection passed between them. They could have been father and son.

Once again the king addressed Tor. "In recognition of your deeds, Sir Tor, I award you three hundred acres and an earldom. May you and your lands prosper."

An earldom was a great honor indeed, I hoped many rich accoutrements came with it. Tor bowed. He was hard put to speak, but the king did not wait for a reply. "Come sup with us," he said, adding, "there is a place here for Twixt also."

And that is how I, once called Dungbeetle, came to dine with the king.

CHAPTER 15

The day had passed quickly, and in the heat of the afternoon, Nimue and I moved to the shallows under the willow tree. Its branches hung around us like delicate green curtains, the sunlight on the water flickering beyond. We wet ourselves thoroughly, and Nimue lay back in the water with a contented sigh. "So lovely here," she murmured, her hair fanning out in the water like seaweed. Her eyes closed. In another moment she would be asleep.

I had no intention of letting that happen. "What about the other two knights?" I prodded. "What were their names? Tor and—?"

"And Pellinore," she replied, with a pointed lack of interest.

"Tell me about them," I coaxed. "Did you follow them, too?"

She shook her head. "Merlin was *so* kind to me that day,"

she said, "and he is so much *sweeter* than he appears, did you know?—that I chose to stay with him instead of chasing after Sir Tor or Sir Pellinore. As it happened," she added, a little smugly, "there was no need to follow either one, because Merlin could see them *any time* he wanted to. He has spells for *everything!*" She said this to herself as much as to me, and the envy in her voice was almost comical. If and when she attained her full powers, they would never equal Merlin's; she had to know that! I reminded myself that she was very young.

"He conjured up visions! And we *watched* them!" she said, with a sidelong glance. "Can *you* do that?"

I balked at the question. "A Lady Must Never Discuss Her Powers," I said, quoting from the Rules. "As you well know."

"Not even with me?" she asked, all innocence. "But, Damosel, we're practically *sisters!*"

"Don't wheedle, Nimue," I scolded. "And don't pout. You look like a child of seventy!"

"You and your Rules! You are *such* an old stickler!" she complained, splashing her feet in the Lake. *And you are such a whiny baby!* I yearned to say. But arguing with Nimue was futile. She heard what she wanted to hear and ignored the rest, so I held my tongue.

For a moment she pouted and I listened to the waves breaking in the distance. Then I said, "Tell me about Tor and Pellinore, won't you?"

"Oh, all right," she said, wringing out her long, black-green hair and fastening it atop her head with a couple of twigs. "Did I mention that Merlin and I spent the day together?"

I shook my head.

"Well, we did," she said. "We sat and talked in the dining hall for the longest time, *hours* after the banquet. Merlin told me about helping Arthur—in his military campaigns, his affairs of state, and even the design of Camelot—and every bit of it was positively *riveting*!

"Then, when we were strolling outside, I happened to wonder about Sir Ablamar of the Marsh, the lord whose lady was beheaded. He had failed to appear at court.

"Merlin smiled very mysteriously and said, 'Would you like to see him?' Of course I said yes.

"The next thing I knew, we were in an herb garden, a secluded little place that smelled of thyme and lavender and seemed to pop up out of *nowhere*. We sat down—there were two chairs there, facing the north wall—and he told me to close my eyes. Then he said something fast and guttural, *completely* unlike his normal speech. The air went very still, the way it does before a storm, and I realized he was casting a spell. But I didn't open my eyes until he told me to. Then he said, 'Look there,' and pointed at the wall.

"Damosel, there were *pictures* playing on the wall, *moving* pictures! Clear and bright as the most *vivid dream*!"

Fancy magic, I thought.

"First came a man on a horse, his face spattered with blood. He was weeping, and when his horse wandered into the marsh, he let it.

"'There is Ablamar,' Merlin told me, 'lost in his grief.'

"The image faded, and then we saw Sir Pellinore, fighting furiously with a knight in the forest. The woman whose bratchet had been taken—"

"The one with the rasping voice?"

"Yes. Merlin said her name was Vivyenne. She stood by, watching the knights, wringing her hands in *acute* distress. They were all real as life! It was *transfixing!*"

I had never heard Nimue gush so. Then again, she was describing some very showy conjuring.

"Pellinore won his duel," she went on, "and he faded away, but a new picture appeared on the wall almost instantly. This time we could see Pellinore riding along a broad highway with Vivyenne. He looked horribly out of sorts, and she was complaining *most* energetically."

"But why? Pellinore rescued her."

Nimue shrugged. "From his expression, he yearned to hood her, as if she were an overexcited falcon. Though he might have preferred to stun her with a large object and fling her over his saddle . . . I'm not certain. In any case, he refrained," she said, with a touch of disappointment. "They appeared soon after, and Pellinore presented her to the king."

"His quest sounds like more of a trial than an adventure."

"Yes."

"And Vivyenne's dog? Was it ever returned to her?"

Nimue smiled mischievously. "I will tell you—*if* you give me a cup of gooseberry wine."

"You are not really old enough for wine," I said, though in fact the Rules are not as clear as they might be on the subject of drinking ages.

"I'm almost a hundred and ten!" she protested. "That's positively middle-aged!"

Well, thank you very much, I thought. *That makes me ancient!* "Half a cup," I said briskly. "No more."

CHAPTER 16

Before long Nimue had consumed far more than half a cup of gooseberry wine, and so had I. The sun was now as orange as a daylily, and we strolled to a hillock overlooking the ocean to watch it set. We got there just as it turned the horizon crimson. An instant later, after one last blaze of yellow-green, it sank, leaving sea and sky to their own devices.

"Now, where was I?" asked Nimue, plucking a strand of sea grass and threading it through her fingers.

"The bratchet?" I ventured.

"Oh yes. Well," she said, "in a moment. There is more I must tell you about Merlin."

Your new favorite subject, I thought.

"The next day I woke early, and the very *instant* my eyes opened, I remembered his magical images of Pellinore and Vivyenne," she said. "It was a glorious morning, so I decided to revisit the little herb garden. Oddly, though, I could not find it."

He conjured it up, I thought, *hoping to impress you. As if you didn't know.*

"So then I decided to find *Merlin*," she went on, "which was nearly as difficult. I looked high and low, and after asking a guard, a page, and a dairyman, I found him in the kitchen, watching the bakers knead their dough."

This struck me as an odd thing for a sorcerer to be doing and I said so.

"I thought so, too, at the time," said Nimue. "But now that I know him better, I have learned that his curiosity about the making of things is *boundless*. He can spend an entire day watching a spider spin its web! I have heard him pose questions to a leech about bleeding, to a weaver about silk, and to a mason about the placing of stones, each time as though he had *long* been practicing the craft himself! I had the distinct impression that he would remember *every single thing* he was told." She shook her head in droll disbelief.

"After we exchanged greetings, I told him that I could think of nothing else but the wonderful images he had shown me. He insisted that they had been nothing, a mere trifle. Can you *imagine*?" she exclaimed, giving me no time to reply. "He is *so* brilliant!"

Not when it comes to flattery, I thought.

"He knows *everything* there is to know about the king," she went on. "*Fascinating* things. The circumstances of Arthur's birth, for example. According to Merlin, Uther would stop at nothing to get what he wanted."

Uther was Arthur's father, a powerful king. The moment he

set eyes on the beautiful Lady Igraine, wife of Lord Gorlois, he resolved to have her for his queen, and to this end he called upon Merlin. The wizard agreed to help him and used some very cunning magic to bring Igraine to Uther's bed. In payment, he demanded their child. Igraine's husband, Lord Gorlois, died in battle, she and Uther were married, and the day after Arthur was born, Merlin took him away.

He had arranged for a good-natured knight called Sir Ector to raise Arthur so that after Uther's death, when the kingdom collapsed, the boy would be safe. Then, when the time was right, Merlin used his magic to help Arthur claim the throne.

It was a dark, wonderful story, much told in the fairy world though denied vehemently by converts to the new religion, who preferred their own magic tales.

"I know the story," I said.

"Then you know that his accomplishments did not stop there," Nimue pressed on. "Once Arthur had the crown, Merlin made sure that the northern kings swore fealty—this after years of battles, skirmishes, and constant unrest. Not only that, he kept the Saxons at bay—no mean feat, as they are *hideously* warlike (or so Merlin says). If you ask me," she added, "*he* might as well be king, for he is *much* more powerful than Arthur; everybody knows that." She said this with such awful smugness that I wanted to lock her up in a tree.

Instead I changed the subject. "But what about the dog, Nimue? Did Sir Tor ever bring it back to Camelot?"

"Yes, yes," she replied, reluctant to leave the subject of Merlin and his godlike charms. "Both he and Sir Pellinore fulfilled their quests and returned during the midday meal.

"First came Tor. He arrived with the white dog *and* a dwarf, and Merlin made a prediction about him that caused an uproar—he said Tor would accomplish great things and become one of Arthur's best-loved knights! The poor boy was so overcome that he nearly choked. Oh, and Arthur made him an earl."

"Good for him," I said. "And Pellinore?"

"Rode in during sweetmeats with the Lady Vivyenne. He described finding her and subduing her kidnapper, the knight Ontelake—just as I had seen it in the garden. Then he said, 'The remainder of the quest was uneventful, Sire,' which struck me as *incredibly* charitable, considering Vivyenne's behavior."

"And what of her?" I asked. "Any more complaints?"

"Not a one," said Nimue. "The instant Pellinore finished, the bratchet, who had been sitting with the dwarf, broke away and positively *hurled* itself at Vivyenne. It nearly knocked her down—not that she minded. 'Snowflake! Snowflake! My darling little Snowie!' she cried—very piercingly, I might add—falling to her knees and exchanging kisses with the dog. It was the most *extraordinary* display!

"Upon being told that she and her beloved Snowflake would never, ever be parted again—*if* she remained reasonably quiet—she fell silent and sat down to dine. And do you know the dog actually sat on her lap at the table?! She gave it bits of her own food!" Nimue rolled her eyes in mock wonder at Vivyenne's behavior.

"As for Pellinore," she went on, "he rejoined his friends with visible relief the moment Arthur gave him leave."

Arthur? I thought. *Are you on such easy terms with him already?* "It's growing dark," I observed, suddenly wishing her away, and she stretched, smiling.

As we got to our feet, she said, "Before the feast ended,

Pellinore, Gawaine, and Tor took vows to serve the king, help those in need, and show mercy always. It was all very solemn." She took my arm. "You know how people are," she added as we turned back toward the Lake. "Whenever they truly enjoy themselves, they end up by making promises."

"Well, I have truly enjoyed myself," I said, "but I won't promise anything—except a warm welcome on your next visit. I hope it will be soon." I said this with strained enthusiasm, but Nimue never took note.

"I hope so, too," she said, "though I will be away for a time. . . . Did I mention that Merlin is taking me to Brittany next week?"

Did I mention that you are deeply annoying? I thought. *Stay away from him!*

"He wants to show me his birthplace and some other things that he holds dear."

"Nimue—" I began, a hint of warning in my voice.

"Yes, Damosel?" she said, looking at me wide-eyed. For an instant I felt that she was daring me to object to her dalliance with Merlin. *If I do*, I thought, *she'll only want him more.* "Never mind," I said.

Besides, I told myself, he was the mightiest wizard of our time. She could beguile him, but could she coax real magic out of him? Doubtful.

We embraced. "It was lovely to see you," she said.

"And you," I replied. I expected her to leave by water, as she had come, but she melted into the air, which suddenly glowed with fireflies.

Nice trick, I thought, wondering where she'd gotten it.

But of course I knew.

PART THREE

In Which Damosel Makes a Promise

It was not until late summer that I heard what Nimue had done to Merlin. I was outraged. I knew my cousin was heartless and that Merlin's power had drawn her like a lodestone, so I had half expected to hear that she had winkled a few secrets out of him—harmless ones, like the firefly trick—as proof of his affection. But what she had done was much, much worse. She had persuaded him to teach her some very strong magic, and then used it to lock him in an underground cavern near the sea. The spell was so powerful that Merlin himself had not yet broken it, so in the cave he remained, doubtless contemplating his folly.

Poor Merlin, I thought sadly. *You should have disappeared when you saw her coming.* Then I thought, *No, I should have warned him.* But I had chosen to heed *The Rule of*

Non-interference in the Romantic Affairs of Other Ladies. And that, I had to admit, was one of *my* worst mistakes.

❧

A water vision and a great deal of bird chatter had led me to this windswept place, a scrubby hillock on a cliff overlooking the Narrow Sea. To the north was Tintagel, the great fortress where Uther's wife, Igraine, had borne Arthur. Across the choppy waters lay France, where Merlin had often gone to parley with kings and warlords on Arthur's behalf.

Beneath me, in an underground chamber, was Merlin himself—or so I hoped. I tapped on the rounded, stony mound at the center of the hillock (it was very much like knocking on an oversized bald head) and raised my voice above the wind. "Merlin?" I called. "Are you there?"

"Nimue?" Hearing his muffled reply, I pressed my ear to the stone. "Nimue?" he repeated eagerly, hopefully.

"No, it's Damosel," I said, hating to disappoint him. "I've come to help you. I'm going to try some releasing spells. One of them should work."

"Don't bother," he said flatly.

"What do you mean?"

"The spell she cast—that I taught her—cannot be reversed."

"What?!" For one wild moment I thought he was jesting.

"I warned her," he said. "When I saw what she meant to do, I told her what would happen. But . . ." His sigh was loud enough for me to hear.

At that moment I positively hated my cousin and her

blithe, willful ignorance. "It can't be true!" I protested. "I'll find her and bring her back here, and—"

"That would not change anything."

I struggled with the notion that Merlin was powerless. "Surely there must be—"

He cut me short. "Damosel, I will never leave this place."

A jackdaw screeched. The wind slapped at my face and my eyes burned. Anger, shame, and sorrow did the rest; I began to cry.

"I will tell you what you *can* do," he said after a moment, "if you are willing."

I wiped my nose and cleared my throat. "I am more than willing."

After a moment he said, "You Ladies of the Lake have always been resourceful, good at finding your way around obstacles. And your shape-shifting skills are excellent. There aren't many in the spirit world who can dissolve into mist, or enshroud like fog, as well as you do."

Well, that's true, I thought. *I've certainly done my share of the mist and fog things.*

"And you're persistent," he went on. "The way you overcome opposition like water does, wearing away stone, is a good trait . . . usually. . . ." His voice trailed off.

Except when it forces you to give up powerful secrets, I thought, certain that Nimue, the dreadful girl, had done exactly that.

"Once she has made up her mind," Merlin went on, "a Lady is a strong adversary—equal to almost any challenge."

Ashamed for my cousin yet again, I cringed and stammered, "I—I am so sorry about Nimue."

"I was not thinking of her," said Merlin sharply, "but of you."

"Me?" I blurted.

"Listen well," he said, and I did.

The events of the day required serious reflection, so when Merlin was finished, I hastened back to my Lake and immersed myself at once.

The wizard had said many startling things.

After more kind words about the Ladies of the Lake, he had gone on to speak of Arthur. "Good-hearted to a fault," he said fondly. "Looks for the best in everyone. Kind, merciful, stalwart, fair . . . terrible qualities in a king."

What?

"Terrible because they make him vulnerable," Merlin continued. "Arthur does not want to believe his half sisters hate him, but they do. Margause will never forgive him for killing her husband, Lot, and depriving her of the chance to be queen. Morgan Le Fay loathes him just as much—she sees him as a usurper who appeared without warning and shamelessly stole her place. Yet he treats them well. As for Mordred, he is fast becoming what Margause has wanted ever since Lot died—someone who detests Arthur and dreams of destroying him."

Mordred was Margause's youngest son, and there had always been gossip about his parentage. It was rumored that Arthur had fathered the boy unknowingly on Margause, that she had seduced him long before he became king. On learning of it—and wanting nothing to do with the child—Arthur had shipped him off to one of the northern islands.

"But Arthur sent Mordred away."

"Not far enough," said Merlin. "He will come back. And then . . ."

"And then?"

"I will not be there to help. And Arthur will need it, I assure you. Mordred, Margause, Morgan—they will cause him more travail than all the Saxons, Jutes, and Picts put together."

I was about to ask about Margause's other sons, the four who were at court, when Merlin said, "So. Will you take my place?"

I was too surprised to reply.

"You are the only one who can, Damosel. Say you will. Please."

My place is in the Lake, I thought, *not at court!* Leaving my home was the last thing I wanted to do, and I searched my mind frantically for a Rule that would prevent me. But of all the prohibitions restraining us—from a Rule against summoning double rainbows midweek to a Rule against remaining completely dry for three consecutive days—I could not think of one that obtained. Those that did come to mind—*The Rule of Service to Worthy Kings, The Ounce of Prevention Rule,* and myriad Rules about helping those in need—supported Merlin's request. There were Rules governing travel, decorum, and personal hygiene, etiquette, accountability, and footwear— everything, it seemed, except the one I required.

So I agreed, and Merlin made me swear. I took an oath to protect Arthur that was so long and binding it made my palms dry, and when it was done, Merlin said, "Arthur is weary of battle. His dearest wish is for peace. I would have helped him achieve it, if not for—" He broke off, no doubt because he was picturing my beautiful, untrustworthy cousin, Nimue the Disgraceful. "He still might, with your help," Merlin concluded.

A worthy goal, I thought, remembering the day when I gave Arthur Excalibur, his expression when he learned that the sword's death blow would cause no pain. Only a peace-loving man would show such relief. But his world was combative, it always had been. *He may subdue his foes*, I reflected, *but will he change their natures?*

"I do not like to think it is impossible," said Merlin, as if he had read my mind.

I wondered. Still, I told him I would do my best for Arthur.

"I know you will," he replied.

Now, mulling over our last exchange, my blood cooled, my breathing quieted, and my fears slowly drifted away. The wind, so much gentler here than on the cliffs near Tintagel, touched the Lake like a soothing hand. I would never be a great mage like Merlin, but I could help Arthur, and I would. My mind becalmed, I floated, thinking nothing. Then—so slowly that I could not say when it happened—I entered the dream state where visions appeared.

More time passed, and more, and then it came: I saw Arthur, alone with Morgan Le Fay, placing a long, narrow wooden box into her eager hands. The jeweled sword in the box lay in a scabbard of fine-grained dragon skin. Seeing it, Morgan bared her teeth in a smile worthy of a feral cat.

No wonder she is smiling, I thought, for I knew the sword well.

It was Excalibur.

My eyes flew open. Had Arthur just given his sword to Morgan Le Fay? How could he do something so foolish? All Merlin's warnings about Arthur's vulnerability came back to me as I shot to the surface of the Lake. *If he wants to kill himself,* I thought, *he has made a fine beginning.*

CHAPTER 18

Tor was away buying horses when it happened. I should have gone with him. But out of laziness or stupidity I did not, and before I knew it her spell was cast. One minute I was juggling corncobs near the stable in a patch of sunlight, the castle urchins watching. The next they were skittering away like mice from a cat and there she was, a slight woman richly dressed, her narrow eyes probing mine—the king's sister Morgan Le Fay. When the servants spoke of her their voices dropped. She was faithless, she shared her favors with her husband's young friend Sir Accolon, and Sir Uriens, getting on in years, never guessed. They said it was witchery, that she had the Dark Sight and other powers too terrible to name. She was not well liked.

She had never even looked my way before.

Now she raised her palm. The corncobs stopped in midair. I gaped.

"Twixt?" she asked. I nodded.

"You must do something for me," she said. Her voice was smooth, like the touch of silk. "Tell no one lest I turn you to stone." It was a threat but she could have been whispering endearments, and I prickled all over. The sensation was sweet, strongest when her eyes held mine. I nodded again. There was no denying her.

"Good," she said. The corncobs fell, she beckoned, and I followed.

She dismissed the women in her chambers, then unlocked a cupboard, drawing out a long narrow box. It was gilded, fastened tight, and heavier than it looked. I had to use both arms to hold it.

"Carry this to Sir Accolon," she said. "He awaits it in the Summer Country." She led me to the window. "See the donkey?" A little gray animal stood in the courtyard. It wore a child-sized saddle. *For me*, I thought numbly. Her hand touched my shoulder. It, too, was heavier than it looked.

I bowed my head. It seemed I could no longer speak.

"The donkey knows the way," she said. "Now go."

It was like a fever dream, no telling what was real and what was sorcery. I knew I traveled very far and very fast, the box like a wooden babe cradled in my arms. The donkey trotted on both day and night, passing through unfamiliar country without food or sleep or water. Then we crossed a wide plain and halted before a striped pavilion. I sat there waiting, for what I did not even care.

A man came out. He was gentry, dressed in brown. A black stone on a cord glinted at his throat. I had seen such a stone hanging from Morgan's ear. This could have been its twin.

"Morgan sent you?" he asked, a dull craving in his eyes. He did not need to tell me he was Accolon.

I nodded.

"Good," he said, taking the box from me. I felt a pang of loss so sharp it made me groan. And this not even knowing what the box contained.

"Tell her I will soon be with her," he said. He opened the box, revealing a sword fit for a king. A glimpse was all I got. The donkey's ears pricked up, heeding some distant command, and we were away.

CHAPTER 19

I had never imagined I would have to keep my promise to Merlin so quickly, but then I had never dreamed that Excalibur would fall into Morgan's hands, either, and now it had.

She had taken the scabbard, too. Imbued with magic strong enough to stanch Arthur's blood, it had virtually ensured his safety; in Morgan's hands it spelled calamity.

I stood in the shallows, thinking miserably of how easily the king might be killed. He and his knights loved swordplay and would hoist their weapons at the slightest excuse—a wager, a dare, an idle moment threatening boredom. Some traitorous opponent—or an innocent one, under Morgan's spell—could wound Arthur at any time. The thought was a barb, stabbing me cruelly with every breath, yet I was unsure of what to do. Addled and irresolute, I realized how languorous my life had been until this moment. With endless time at my disposal, I had never had to hurry.

Well, you do now, I told myself, hurtling onto shore. *Find Excalibur and the scabbard! Use the spell!*

The finding spell had been an afterthought, cast hastily as a precaution. I had told myself I was being fussy, even wasting valuable magic, yet I had gone ahead anyway, giving the sword the ability to summon me if I reached out to it. Now I was glad I had taken the trouble.

I recited the spell so fast that it sounded like gibberish. The response was slow in coming. When it did, and I heard the high keening, like a hawk's cry, I went damp with relief. As long as I could hear it, I would find Excalibur.

I stepped into my caïque, a pretty little boat better suited to local meanderings than a long journey. *It will do,* I told myself, steering north. *It will have to.*

But will I? Despite Merlin's encouragement ("You are more powerful than you know"), I would never be Morgan's equal. She was an icy, cunning enchantress who made Nimue look like a dingle fairy, and the prospect of coming up against her made me quail.

But I could not turn back. I had sworn to protect the king.

"A Lady Always Keeps Her Promises" was a Rule I would not break.

And so, upon reaching the Lake's northernmost shore, I continued to follow Excalibur's call, gliding up through the waterways of Dumnorium and eastward, away from the sea. There was a water pathway going west, where Merlin was imprisoned, and when I crossed it, still heading north and east, the air changed, becoming softer, more fragrant. Along with Excalibur's call I heard a flock of swallows extolling the local millet and knew I was in farmland. The fields were rich with grain, the countryside impossibly lush and green, but I had not seen a familiar landmark since the waterways crossed.

"Where are you taking me?" I murmured. A distant, keening cry was my only answer.

I urged my little boat on, pleased to discover how swiftly it could go. Before long the gentle hills by the stream smoothed out entirely, becoming a vast, flat, scrubby plain under the enormous sky. It looked as if it had been put there for the sole purpose of displaying some great wonder.

And that cannot be far from the truth, I thought, for when I saw them, the Great Stones were wonderful indeed. At a distance they were like a ring of ancient sages, tilting toward one another as if trading wisdom. Closer up they were darker and more majestic, almost forbidding.

It was easy to picture Merlin standing in the center of the stones, leading the harvest rites. "He presides every year," Nimue had told me, in the admiring, somewhat possessive tone she used when speaking of him early on, before she—

I stopped myself. On leaving Merlin, I had resolved not to dwell on Nimue's faults, for doing so invariably led me back to my own. I might not be greedy for magic, or wily, or cold-hearted, but my shortcomings had helped my cousin, there was no escaping it. I was timid, terrified of making a fuss, and completely without ambition; so awkward, shy, and homebound that I had declined an invitation to the king's wedding; and wholly dependent on the Rules to guide my life.

It's a good thing there is no Rule forbidding self-pity, I thought morosely. *If there were, you'd be breaking it all the time.* With this, I found that I had come far beyond the Great Stones and was traveling a stream in the depths of a forest.

A deer and her fawn watched me solemnly as I passed. Far ahead, a cloud of white butterflies disappeared in a shaft of sunlight. The stream, as if growing impatient, pulled me out of the trees into the brightness of day with something like urgency. When I stopped blinking, I saw barley and wheat fields, edged by a cluster of round thatched huts—a small village. Beyond it was a turreted castle, pennants luffing in the breeze. Given the time since I had passed the Great Stones and the lush fields and gentle green swells of the terrain, I might very well be in the Summer Country. The region, so called because the king liked to move his court here in the heat of the summer, was only a few days from Londinium, the largest city in his realm.

I have come very far, I thought, *and so has Excalibur.*

At that very moment I heard the sword again. Its call was nearly drowned out by cries of excitement, shouts of encouragement, and the harsh clanging whine of metal on metal. My palms went dry with apprehension. Men were dueling.

I found them in a dusty arena, facing off with drawn swords before a hushed crowd. Both were masked. I wondered why but put the question aside—there were more pressing matters to consider, such as whether I could stop them from killing each other. I had already obscured myself; now I eased through the spectators until I was a stone's throw from the combatants. A party of knights and ladies watched the contest from under a canopied platform. If Morgan Le Fay was among them, I did not see her.

Meanwhile, the men—one in a blue tunic, the other in

brown—circled each other wearily, chests heaving. From the look of it they had been fighting for some time. The man in blue was bleeding hard, and there were bright red splashes around him in the dust. He swayed and almost fell but managed to remain on his feet by propping himself up on his sword.

The man in brown approached his weakened opponent, wielding Excalibur. *There it is!* I thought, noting with pride the way its jewels flashed in the sun. *Such a handsome sword!* My whole being seemed to unclench. Seeing it in the king's hands—and surely the man in brown was Arthur—I knew he was safe. I allowed myself a quiet sigh of relief.

But in the next moment the man in blue, still using his sword as a prop, drew himself up to his full height. The pommel was nicely worked, studded with unusually fine gems. The largest, a ruby, was truly of the first water.

Excalibur! I thought. *He has Excalibur also!*

That was impossible.

I looked from one man to the other. Their swords were exactly the same. I could make very little sense of what I was seeing, but I knew there was magic at work here, all of it bad.

The fight resumed. The man in brown lunged and struck, connecting with his opponent's sword, and with a sound like breaking glass, the blade came apart and fell to the ground. The man in blue looked down at his useless weapon, his jaw tightening. *Ginger stubble,* I noted, while the crowd pressed forward.

There was only one true Excalibur, and it was invincible. That meant the broken sword was a copy of the one I had made—with none of its powers.

Recalling my vision of Arthur and Morgan, I saw again the way her expression changed when she took Excalibur, going from surprise to naked anticipation. *How quickly she devised a plan to murder him!* I thought. *She had so little time!* I could only guess at the magic Morgan had used to lure her brother here, but the false Excalibur and the masked duel were her doing, I was sure of it.

I looked again at the man in blue. The upper half of his face was masked, but the set of his jaw and his coppery three-day beard convinced me that I knew him.

"Arthur?" I whispered. Hearing me, he turned his head. It was all the proof I needed, and I began to cast a spell at once.

CHAPTER 20

"Yield," said the man in brown. The crowd fell silent.

"Upon my honor," replied Arthur, "I will not."

"Then you must die."

A horse nickered. A dog whined. Nobody on two legs made a sound. "Strike me," Arthur said quietly, "and live with the consequences."

Hearing these words, the man in brown hesitated. At the same time there were scattered cries from the crowd. "Do not! He is unarmed!" protested one man. "Shame! Shame!" shouted a few others. A young noblewoman in the stands shrieked and fainted, falling against the woman beside her. She, not to be outdone, promptly fainted, too. Many in the stands averted their eyes.

The man in brown raised Excalibur with both hands, preparing to strike.

Now my hindering spell took effect, and the man's arms, rendered useless, flopped to his sides. While his mouth worked in silent terror, Excalibur left his hands. It hung in the air, as if awaiting orders.

"Go to your master!" I whispered.

It was lovely to see the weapon float over to Arthur, who took hold of it firmly, and I must admit I enjoyed the awed hisses of the villagers, too. Until this moment I had done magic in private, with an audience of (mostly disinterested) birds and fish. Human approbation was surprisingly pleasant.

But if Arthur felt the least bit of awe or exhilaration with this latest turn of events, he did not show it. Perhaps flying swords and dizzying reversals of fortune were humdrum after all his time with Merlin. As for his magic sword, once he had it in hand, he proceeded to scold it.

"You have been gone too long from me, Excalibur," he said, as if the weapon were an errant foot soldier, "and done me harm, too. Now be my ally."

Fairly humming in obedience, the sword dealt the man in brown a ringing, flat-sided wallop to the head that knocked him senseless.

Arthur quickly reclaimed Excalibur's scabbard, which had been hanging from the man's belt, and attached it to his own. With this, the many shallow cuts on the man's body, showing as fine red lines on his tunic, grew thicker and darker, and he began to bleed in earnest. *Doomed*, I thought, guessing that he was some poor, unlucky knight who had crossed Morgan's path at the wrong time, only to fall under her spell.

Meanwhile, Arthur's own bleeding had stopped, and he was standing straighter.

"Now *you* must yield," he said firmly. The man's response was a feeble shake of the head. Arthur ignored it. He pulled off the man's mask, uncovering a face caked with dust and blood.

"Tell me your name," he demanded, but softly.

"I am . . . Accolon of Gaul," the man replied, his eyes still closed, "a knight . . . of King . . . Arthur's court."

Arthur became very still. "How did you come by your sword, Accolon?" he asked.

"The Lady Morgan Le Fay sent it to me. . . ." Accolon's hand went to his neck, and his fingers closed around a dark stone amulet. She had probably given it to him for protection.

"She said I must fight with it and kill every foe, that one of them would be the king. . . . I would kill him unbeknownst. . . . If I did her bidding, she promised to make me king and rule beside me. . . . I . . . I loved her too well. And . . . she swore she loved me."

Arthur pulled off his mask. His face was bitterly sad. "She had you spellbound," he said. This evidence of Morgan's hatred must have been terrible for him to bear. There is no blood hatred in the fairy world, for which I am grateful. It is an ugly thing.

"I suppose. . . ." Accolon's breath caught in his throat and blood bubbled at the corner of his mouth. His eyelids fluttered.

"Do you not know me?" asked Arthur, leaning down. Accolon whispered something, and Arthur brushed the grime from Accolon's eyes.

By now the villagers had encircled the two men and were straining to hear. The gentlefolk in the stands, sensing something unusual, left their seats to join the crowd, which gave way to them grudgingly. I seated myself in the branches of a nearby birch, where only the sparrows noticed.

Accolon's eyes opened at last. When he saw Arthur, he blinked twice, as if trying to alter what he was seeing. An instant passed. Tears sprang into his eyes. "My liege!" he uttered hoarsely. "Is it you . . . ?"

"It is," said Arthur, "though I wish it were otherwise."

"I, too," said Accolon, adding brokenly that he had been a treasonous fool and did not deserve the king's mercy.

"Nevertheless, I grant it," said Arthur. "Morgan is a powerful enchantress. She ensnared us both." He helped Accolon to his feet, propping him up while he addressed the crowd.

"This knight and I fought because we were deceived," he said. "Villainy and magic made us adversaries."

Then Accolon spoke. "Here is the best and bravest knight in all the world . . . and he is your king! Bow to him!" he gasped. "And . . . if he shows you any kindness, count yourselves fortunate . . . as I do." He sank back into Arthur's arms, seeming to shrink as he did so. He had very little time left.

I knew by looking at their faces that everyone believed Accolon, that they would recognize Arthur as their king and kneel to him forthwith. But telling myself that it was for his safety, I cast another spell from my perch in the tree, one that made Arthur appear stronger and nobler than he was. It worked wonderfully well; in no time at all he seemed so majestic and puissant that every soul in the vicinity dropped to the ground as if mowed down by a scythe. Even I was impressed.

I had done it partly for my own pleasure, I admit, but any guilt I felt (was I using unnecessary magic?) was short-lived.

Seeing Arthur reverenced as king after his ordeal made me so giddily happy that I allowed myself to think that even Merlin would approve.

I was still enjoying the glow of successful magic-making when Arthur and Accolon were carried to a nearby hospice. I heard someone say that the nuns were known for their healing skills and dared to think that Arthur would be safe in their care. By nightfall he was visibly stronger.

Not so Accolon. He died later that night, holding Arthur's hand. He was prayed over, laid out, and shrouded, and then Arthur sent him back to Camelot with a message for Morgan. It said, *Your mischief caused Accolon's death; here is his body. As for Excalibur, it is at my side, where it belongs.*

Cheered by the sight of Arthur sleeping peacefully in a quiet, whitewashed cell with Excalibur safely in his grasp, I departed the abbey.

Alas, I left too soon.

CHAPTER 21

The donkey brought me back, trotting all the way. In the castle courtyard it fell stone dead, its body flat on the cobbles.

"Remove the animal," she said, and the stable boys jumped to do her bidding. She looked at me and I hastened to her as if pulled. "You gave him the box?" she asked, her voice like a secret caress. I was weak and parched, lacking the wherewithal to speak, so I nodded.

A goblet of water appeared before me, and she indicated with her chin that I should take it. I drank thirstily, so grateful for this small boon that I nearly sobbed. "What did he say?" she asked.

Much else was lost, but this I remembered. "That he would soon be with you and stay for all eternity." She blushed, her face softening into a different kind of beauty. Accolon's promise pleased her well.

That night she let me sleep outside her chamber. At dawn she called me in to wait for Accolon's return. He came in an oxcart. When she saw the still form in the cart, she gripped my shoulder hard, as if she was falling.

"Is it Arthur?" she whispered. I knew it was not, and surely she did also, for the cart was a rough country thing, made for farming, and only two knights flanked it. The king would not travel so, his body would be carried in state, with—what was the word?—an *entourage*. Grasping the truth, she whispered Accolon's name. Then a groan escaped her, a sound of grief and rage. I hope I never hear its like again.

Still under her spell, wanting only to be with her, I trailed her down to the courtyard, where one of the knights gave her a written message. She stared at the scroll for a long time as if willing the words to change, but here her magic could not help her. "Take him to the chapel yard," she told the knights flatly.

She watched them go, then flicked the scroll away, it turned to chaff on the wind. Then she drew herself up and strode into the castle, straight to the Great Hall. I followed like a pup.

The king's throne was empty, but the queen was there, the court herbalist kneeling before her. From his case of powders and potions he pulled a flask of greenish liquid. This, he promised, would raise her spirits and clear her nose, which was very red. She thanked him listlessly, then commenced to cough.

All this time my lady had been quietly approaching the throne, and at last the queen noticed her.

"Morgan," she said, her eyes suddenly attentive.

"Majesty," replied Morgan with a bow of the head. "I trust you are well?"

"You see how I am." Guinevere sneezed, the sound echoing in the hall. She smiled wanly. "Pour me some of this so I can dose myself," she told one of her ladies, giving her the flask. It must have tasted terrible, she pulled a face when she drank it. She composed herself and looked inquiringly at Morgan.

"My lady, I must ask your leave to return to my own lands," said Morgan. "I have just received word of trouble there—some tedious dispute over livestock. Alas, only I can settle it."

My guts curled at the thought of her absence. *Do not go!* I prayed silently.

"You do know Arthur will be back from the hunt any day now," said the queen. "He will be sorry to find you gone."

"And I will be sorry to miss him," said Morgan smoothly. "But I should leave for home without delay."

"Of course. Go with my blessing," said the queen, sneezing again by way of farewell.

"Thank you, my lady." Morgan bowed, then swiftly left the hall. I could not keep up on my short legs, even running. When at last I reached her I stumbled, treading on her robe. She whirled around. From her face I could have been a dog and she about to kick me.

"Take yourself away," she said. "I have no more use for you." They were harsh words spoken without a trace of sweetness. I stood there dumb as a rock, not wanting to understand.

"Leave me!" she ordered, her voice like a lash.

But I am yours! I thought, staring at her helplessly. She made a sound of disgust and snapped her fingers in my face three times, muttering.

With my eyes locked on hers I felt all my adoration seep away, leaving only confusion. "Go!" she said, flicking her hand dismissively. I had seen her do this to the scroll, destroying it. *She is close to destroying you,* I thought, and a jolt of terror finally set me in motion. I ran from her witlessly, blindly, as fast as my legs would go. If there had been a well in my path I would have fallen in. As it was I backed into an open doorway and tumbled down a set of stairs, landing hard.

That stopped me.

I woke on a stone floor in the dark. Smelling earth and hops, I knew I was in the ale cellar. It was quiet as a tomb in here—*very restful* was my first thought. Then the pain began, the kind that came after a long beating but before the black and blue marks. Every part of me ached.

It was a long while until I dared to move. I did this very very carefully, one limb at a time. I was glad to find my arms and legs still attached, my noggin too, but it was throbbing in a way I did not like one bit. There were imps in there with pickaxes trying to dig their way out, and on my forehead a gobbetty lump with its own very painful tenderness. I sat up slowly, groaning like a bellows.

At last I was upright. *What happened to you?* I asked myself, and at first I did not know. Then I saw her beautiful scowling face, heard her silky voice, and remembered. The memories— my journey, the sword, Accolon, the oxcart with his body, her angry leave-taking—came in a jumble, like memories of a dream. I waited for the heavy, desperate yearning to come too, but it was gone. My heart failed to lurch when I whispered her name.

"Morgan?" I dared to say it again, half expecting the magic to come back. But there was nothing.

I laughed, even as my eyes flooded.

I was alive and in one piece. Her spell was broken.

CHAPTER 22

Protecting Arthur changed me. I had never had much curiosity about the future before, the present being absorbing enough, but after saving the king from Accolon, the question of what came next was often on my mind. This was both unsettling and exciting, like being roused from a lovely dream to put out a fire. And the fire, without a doubt, was Morgan Le Fay.

I began to think of Arthur's half sister as a puzzle I had to solve—and quickly, too—before she could harm him again. I knew a good deal about her already, because the fairy world is small and shrinking, and we all know each other, at least a little; still, I had yet to learn why she hated him so much.

I began by listening to the birds. This was laborious, because birds chatter the way they feed—all the livelong day, and with a marked preference for quantity over quality. So for every little bit I heard about Morgan—that she had left

Camelot two days prior, visited an abbey near the Great Stones, and hurried away—I heard five times as much about wind currents, seeds, worms, flowers, and boys with slingshots. An exchange between a kingfisher, a sedge warbler, and a sparrow hawk told me that Arthur had pursued Morgan when she left the abbey. A pair of hoopoes—more wide-ranging than their cousins and thus more worldly-wise—reported that Morgan had turned herself into a boulder, hiding in plain sight until the poor confounded king was forced to abandon the chase.

"Stone cold," hooted one.

"Rock hard," sang its mate.

I was happier than I should have been to learn of Morgan's escape. On the general principle of Good Riddance to Bad Magic, I felt that the farther she was from Arthur, the better. Then, putting aside the question of why she hated him so, I got ready to enjoy a nice long soak.

Sadly, I did not remain in the Lake, drifting and dreaming to my heart's content, as I had hoped. In fact, I was disallowed any rest at all, for no sooner was I wet than a cloud of visions assailed me like gnats, stinging with hateful persistence. Much as I wanted to ignore them, I could not.

The visions began with Morgan in a windowless room, casting a spell on a fur-trimmed cloak of purple. I saw her drape it around a kitchen girl's shoulders, the poor wide-eyed thing so awestruck that she hardly dared to stroke it. Next I saw the girl's terror when she understood—too late—that the cloak's luxuriant, poisonous folds were smothering her.

What pointless cruelty! I thought as the image of the dying girl faded. But when I saw Morgan place the cloak in a handsome leather chest and send it away with a damsel on a palfrey, I realized three things: the point of her magic had been to make sure the cloak was lethal; Morgan's damsel was taking it to Arthur; and Morgan never did anything pointless.

I sputtered to the surface, remembering my oath to protect the king.

A Lady Always Keeps Her Promises.

"You are giving me no rest," I muttered, making a few hasty preparations for my trip. I had never been to Camelot before and was not eager to go, but I had to reach Arthur before the cloak did.

As I set out (I went as low-lying mist), I reflected that a different, bolder sort of Lady—Nimue the Dreadful, for example—might have established a presence at court or even forged a close personal link with the king. It had happened long ago, I knew, though it had been many centuries since any Lady had ever been as close to a ruler as Merlin had been to Arthur.

I myself had stayed away from Camelot for a few reasons, my fondness for languor and solitude being the first. I would wager that nobody at court had much of either; from all reports Arthur was never idle and seldom alone. And then there was my aversion to people, especially great numbers of them. I had never questioned it. Why should I?

So I had stayed in the fairy world, as close to home as possible, and when I was drawn away, I kept out of sight by becoming a shadow. *There is no gift like obscurity,* I thought, taking comfort in the knowledge that I could remain unseen at Camelot if I wished. But if I was required to show myself in order to accomplish my task, I would. I owed it to Merlin. Besides, I reasoned, Arthur was a good man who would have chosen trustworthy companions. In all likelihood I had no cause to fear them.

It was a timely thought, for here was the end of my journey: Camelot, with its red-dragon pennants, its mighty stone towers, and its beleaguered king.

Nimue had described the court to me at such length, and in such great detail, that I felt I already knew many of its members. But when I reached the Great Hall and saw the people there—scores and scores of them—I quailed, and before my first tremor of shyness had subsided, I became less, not more, visible. From a small cloud of mist I turned into the merest wisp of a shadow.

Much better, I thought with relief. The sight of Arthur, fully recovered and back on his throne, was a relief also. In a blue tunic of very fine weave, and wearing his crown, he sat with the straight-backed posture of a military man, managing to look entirely at ease and formidable at the same time. Indeed, he appeared better in every way than he had in the Summer Country. I had seen it with my own eyes, but it was still hard to believe that he had suffered that harrowing ordeal such a short time ago. He was a strong man.

Drawing closer, I had my first opportunity to scrutinize Guinevere, whose throne was next to his. I had expected her to be young and self-possessed, for Nimue had said as much in her account of the royal wedding. But I was surprised by her beauty (which Nimue, who recognized no beauty but her own, had of course failed to mention). It was striking, in no small part because her eyes and her thick, straight, silky hair were the same color, a deep, luminous amber.

During my approach, Morgan's emissary had been making the sweetest of speeches to Arthur. "Great Majesty," she began, after an acrobatically deep curtsey, "your loving sister Morgan is painfully aware that she has offended you. She burns with remorse, unable to eat or sleep. She insists on keeping her curtains closed, permitting no daylight in her chamber, and sits alone in blackest gloom, ignoring her monkey, neglecting her ferrets, spurning her handmaids.

"She is sick unto death, Majesty—and would already be dead if not for the hope that this modest token might regain your favor. Please accept it and grant your forgiveness! She begs you from the bottom of her deeply repentant heart."

The open chest at her feet held the cloak of my vision—a splendid garment of deep purple velvet, embellished with gilt and trimmed with spotted cat. "Lovely," murmured Guinevere, and Arthur's face softened. (As Merlin said, he was too forgiving of his kin.)

The damsel held it out invitingly to Arthur. "Will you put it on?" she asked. Arthur started to rise. "Don't touch it!" I hissed into his ear—forgetting that he could not see me. He responded by jumping off his throne and whirling around, wild-eyed, as if seized by madness. Guinevere cried out. Her ladies shrank back.

Fearing that he might touch the cloak, I cautioned him again. "Make her try it on, even if she objects. It is poisoned!" And then, because he hesitated, I revealed myself.

By this time everyone in the hall was staring at the king. They knew him as a kind, steady man whose normal behavior did not include leaping about wide-eyed—at least not in public.

When I became visible, all eyes turned to me. It was less unnerving than I had feared.

"Damosel?" the king asked uncertainly.

I nodded. "Make the girl try it on," I insisted.

This he did, over her protests. I wondered if she knew its terrible power, or what would befall her. No matter—the instant she donned the cloak, it burst into flame, consuming her like a dry stick. Guinevere and her women screamed; Arthur watched impassively, but I knew his mind was roiling. Once again Morgan had wounded him with a show of her implacable hatred. It was an ugly spectacle. *But not fatal for him*, I thought. *Not this time.*

The commotion subsided, the ashes were swept away, and I remained visible while Arthur thanked me so profusely that I yearned to flee. "Now I am doubly in your debt," he concluded, smiling. Was he referring to the help I had given him against Accolon? I had kept myself shadowy for the duration, well out of sight. I had whispered to him, though. Had he recognized my voice? Unlikely.

Then I realized he was referring to a promise he had made when I gave him Excalibur: that he would grant me a boon, any favor I desired, in return for the sword. I had never really intended to claim it, nor did I now. "It is my pleasure to help you, Your Majesty," I assured him. *Not to mention my sworn duty.*

"Call me Arthur."

"Arthur."

Guinevere hurried to Arthur's side. "I, too, am grateful!"

she said, taking my hand (hers was soft, white, and far too small for the enormous ruby adorning her thumb). "Won't you stay with us for a fortnight or two?"

It was the last thing I wanted to do, and I was about to demur when Arthur said, "At least remain until tomorrow. You have scarcely been here an hour."

"I really must be going—" I began, but at that moment a small, stocky figure popped out from behind the throne and somersaulted toward us with great speed, landing directly at my feet. There he knelt, his hands clasped as if in prayer, imploring me. He was a dwarf, no bigger than a child of six, but with the watchful, knowing eyes of someone much older.

Guinevere laughed. "Twixt wants you to stay, too," she said. "See how he pleads?"

"Our jester," added Arthur. "A fine fellow."

I was already missing my Lake, and the thought of an extended absence made my fingertips shrivel. But when the dwarf Twixt added his request to Arthur's and Guinevere's and the skin between my toes began to itch, I realized—with deep chagrin—that I could not refuse. All unknowingly, the royal couple and their jester had managed to invoke an obscure directive from *The Rules Governing the Ladies of the Lake: The Rule of Two and a Half.*

According to this Rule (which to my mind is completely useless, though it may have served some strange purpose in the past), a Lady cannot spurn any request made by two and a half people. She must obey it without question.

Twixt, who was exactly half Arthur's size, still knelt before me. "If you insist," I said.

PART FOUR

In Which Damosel Rescues a Knight in Distress

If I had known what would befall me when I left Camelot, I might have lingered there far beyond my welcome. As it was, my yearning for the Lake was so strong that I made my excuses to Arthur and Guinevere the following morning. After many warm farewells, I was happy to be cloaked in mist and drifting down a stream in the Forest of Arroy, on my way home.

It was unusually warm for winter, and the birds were singing lustily about that wonderful moment—coming soon! coming very soon!—when some nice, juicy earthworms would appear, blissfully unaware that they were breakfast. Then I heard a very different sound—harsh, guttural, rhythmic—punctuating their song. *Not a bird*, I thought as the noise grew louder. Another moment and I reached its source, a young man sitting on the stream bank, pounding his thighs and groaning furiously.

"A pox on her and all her kin!" he cried. "May her hair fall out and her teeth, too! May her nose sprout bulbous festering warts that explode without warning!" He continued to curse in this lively fashion until I interrupted him.

"Who is this woman you so dislike?" I inquired. "What terrible thing has she done to you?"

He yelped in surprise (and perhaps fear, for I had appeared suddenly and was very wet) before he was able to reply.

"She . . . she is the Lady Ettard," he said, "of beauteous aspect and foul disposition. Though my master Sir Pelleas loves her with all his heart, she spurns his every advance, deriding him with the most vigorous contempt! And he"—he wiped his nose with his hand, sniffling energetically—"he bears it meekly! Without complaint! Until yesterday, that is . . ."

"What happened then?" I asked, fascinated. From his description, the Lady Ettard was very much like my disgraceful cousin Nimue. I felt extremely sorry for Sir Pelleas.

"He discovered her with another knight, one who had falsely sworn to help him with his suit. Seeing them asleep together, my master felt a strong impulse to kill them. 'I wanted to, Ralphus,' he told me. 'I left them twice, and when I returned the third time, my sword was drawn.'

"He is a noble soul, gentle-hearted as well as tall and manly, so he did not behead them. He only left his naked sword across their throats as a mild reproof before taking to his bed. He says he would rather die than live without the Lady Ettard's love! He is doomed!" With this he broke into a pathetic rush of sobs and curses.

The tender skin between my toes tickled—was this turning into a chronic condition?—so I knew there was a Rule that applied. I searched my mind. The answer came slowly, and I was pleased to remember it, for *The Rule of Recompense for Mercy Unobserved* is just as obscure as *The Rule of Two and a Half*.

"Take me to him," I said.

I shall never forget my first sight of Pelleas. He lay on a cloak in a little fen, with his eyes closed and his hands clasped on his chest. His handsome face was so still that he could have been carved on a tomb. Only the tears trickling from his eyes betrayed a spark of life.

Perhaps it was his helplessness or his mute suffering, but the sympathy I had felt while learning of his travails now deepened. Yes, I was following a Rule, but even without it, I would have tried to rescue Sir Pelleas, as urgently as if the fate of my world depended upon it.

First I cast a sleeping spell on him, a mild one of brief duration. (*No waste of magic there!*) Then I asked Ralphus the way to the Lady Ettard, and after likening her to a poisonous toad and a cowpat, he told me.

Her castle was easy to find, for it was the only one in the vicinity and quite grand, with two stories, seven windows, and a duck pond. Inside, the stone floors were littered with fur pelts and lapdogs. The presence of two lady's maids further attested to her wealth, as did her earrings—pearls the size of quail eggs that made my throat dry with envy. As I suspected, she was beautiful, with lavish dark curls, a straight nose, and fine, disapproving eyebrows.

I called up my glamour (the regal, implacable kind) and

stood before her until she was suitably intimidated, which only took a moment. Then I said, "Come with me."

She followed without a murmur, and soon we were in the forest. When we reached the fen and she saw Pelleas prostrate and still, she sighed impatiently, as if he had chosen to lie there out of sloth, not heartbreak.

"He is dying of love for you," I said.

"He will not be the first," she replied dismissively. Once again I was reminded of Nimue. *Heartless,* I thought. *No wonder Ralphus hates her.*

Until that moment I had been unsure of what to do, but seeing her lack of pity, I remembered a love reversal spell. I had never expected to use it—it was powerful and called for a good deal of magic. Until Nimue's disgraceful behavior with Merlin, I had hardly thought about love spells, or love, for that matter.

The sight of handsome, heartsick Pelleas changed all that.

I told myself that I was not being wasteful, I was simply obeying *The Rule of Recompense for Mercy Unobserved.* Pelleas had restrained himself from killing the Lady Ettard and her companion though they had betrayed him (mercy unobserved); he would stop loving her, while she fell hopelessly in love with him (recompense).

It all seemed perfectly reasonable.

First I woke Pelleas. Before his eyes were fully open, I cast the spell on him and the lady. To my delight, it took effect at once. He sat up, wide awake, and regarded her with indifference, not adoration.

And Ettard? Now she was the adoring one, first requesting, then imploring, his forgiveness. Her pleas were futile. Pelleas averted his eyes and shook his head, refusing her far more gently than she had refused *him*, if Ralphus was to be believed. Despite her tears he did not relent.

Having seen the misery she had caused, I could not help thinking he was justified, but when he got to his feet, I forgot about Ettard altogether. I hardly even noticed when she left us, for now my attention had turned to him. He was far more interesting.

"My lady, I am most grateful." He spoke the words a little haltingly, and I knew he meant them.

Noting his thick, dark hair, his blunt nose, and his direct demeanor and finding them all to my liking, I said, "I am pleased to help you," and was rewarded with a smile so warm that the rest of the world simply dropped away. We might have been standing inside an enchanted circle.

I did not even think of reading his mind or casting a spell—at that moment I could hardly remember my own name. Instead I simply looked into his eyes, which were bluer than Metite's finest sapphires, thinking, *I want this moment to go on forever.* A moment later I thought, *Well, maybe not forever,* because for some reason he was telling me more about Lady Ettard's cruelty than I ever wished to know. "I hate her as much as I loved her, thank God," he declared.

"No," I replied without hesitation, "thank me."

He blinked, almost as if he were waking again.

"You will be happier when you forget her," I said, wanting him to forget her at once, needing him to grasp the urgency of it. *For both of us!* I thought, more than a little dumbfounded by this surge of emotion.

He looked at me as if he understood. Then he said, "You are right."

They were the best three words I had ever heard.

"I love you," I told him, stepping closer. "Come away with me."

He took my hand, and his touch was like the granting of a long-held, secret wish. "I will," he said.

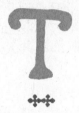

CHAPTER 24

Now I am often at the king's side, serving his bread and pouring his wine. When he bathes I scrub his back as hard as I can. He likes that very much. He also likes my tumbling and my juggling. Practice has improved them.

My situation is better in other ways. My rags are gone, replaced by silk. I wear soft calfskin boots made by the queen's own shoemaker. And when she gives me a rose I carry it in my teeth, for they are cleaner now, no longer brown.

Not so long ago I was still bound by magic to Morgan Le Fay. One day she tired of me and ordered me to go. I could not, for I was hers; that was all I wanted to be. No matter. She cut the ties between us with one snap of her fingers. First I was disenchanted, then terrified. I ran like a chicken trying to fly.

The next day I awoke in the ale cellar. I was bruised but unbewitched, and Morgan was gone.

Free of her and her witchcraft I became myself again.

No, that is not true. I became a happier self.

My spirits rose like a lark on the wing, and the voices in my head told me I should be grateful, that the God of Luck himself had smiled on me.

I believed it and was grateful.

In the days following her departure I nodded and smiled like any ordinary soul. I even laughed at a joke. The sound came out like a bark, startling me along with everybody else, but the feeling was pure pleasure. *I must have more of this*, I thought, *and soon*.

That day I started juggling again. It was corncobs first, then apples, then any old thing I could find. The skill came back quickly, it was like pulling it out of my pocket, and by afternoon a cluster of castle tykes was watching my every move.

A day later I remembered an old trick. With two turnips and a rolling pin in the air I tripped, then pretended to fall. But instead of going down I leaped up as if I had springs in my shoes and caught everything in the nick of time. There was laughter and applause. I bowed, grinning like a fool.

It was a fine moment. The day could only get better with the return of Sir Tor, and to my joy he came riding into the courtyard at noontime. I was so happy I turned a cartwheel. It was a good one, too, ending with a bow.

"A handsome greeting, Twixt!" he said, jumping off his horse. I had forgotten how tall he was until he stood over me, a tower true to his name. Bending from his great height, he clapped me on the shoulder. "How have you fared these past few days?" he asked.

"Well enough," I said. "Juggling a little." I would tell him about Morgan Le Fay later.

"Juggling! Is that why you have an audience?" He cocked his head at the children, they had scrambled away but not too far.

I shrugged. "They have nothing better to do."

"How could you hide your talents from me?" he cried in mock anger. "I must have a demonstration later, what do you say?"

I said yes and reached up to loosen his horse's girth. It was a stretch as always. I cursed under my breath. I would never be a proper squire.

"Leave that," he said, beckoning to a young groom called Amren. He quickly led the horse away. "Come with me."

I followed him into the castle. The first guard we met took us directly to the king. He was in an antechamber alone, reading. I had not been so close to him since the day I first came to Camelot. He looked none too cheerful, but he brightened when he saw Tor and stood to greet him. I hung back.

The two put their heads together, speaking very softly. The king was grave, so was Tor. I could not hear them very well, but I could see that the king was putting many questions to my friend. Something told me they were not about horses. I gave in to my curiosity, drawing as close as I dared. It was one of those times when I was glad to be small. They hardly noticed.

I thought I heard the king say the word *sister*, and when Tor nodded, the king asked, "You did? Where?"

"Near the Forest Perilous," said Tor, "riding as if chased by demons."

"I suppose I should be glad she is gone," said the king, almost to himself. Tor tilted his head in agreement.

They could only be speaking of Morgan Le Fay. *May we be rid of her always and ever,* I prayed, *until the end of time!* The notion that the God of Luck might boot her out was thrilling and I snickered. Loudly. I clapped my hand over my mouth too late. They both turned and stared.

"You are merry today, Twixt," said the king unmerrily.

"I . . . I beg pardon, Sire! It is only that . . . I am so happy to see my master, it has made me . . . almost giddy!"

"You share my high opinion of Tor, do you?"

There was no need to lie about that. I nodded vigorously.

"Twixt welcomed me back in a most unusual manner, Sire," said Tor, and I heard mischief in his voice. "Will you show the king how you greeted me, Twixt?"

My mouth fell open. It was one thing to impress the castle urchins, but the king? He was watching me expectantly, I could not say no, so I said yes. Between reaching a spot on the left side of the room and dusting my hands on the soles of my shoes, I lost my fear. *The king wants a little distraction,* I thought, *just like the children.* I decided to surprise him.

With a deep breath I was off, turning one, two, three cartwheels in a row, finishing directly before His Majesty—not even panting, I am proud to say. I bowed.

"Well done!" cried the king. He smiled broadly.

"Can you juggle with the same finesse?" Tor asked me.

I shrugged. "For you to say, master."

Tor tossed me his dagger and the king threw me a silver goblet. After all my practice with corncobs and apples and horseshoes, keeping only two things in the air was as easy as kiss my hand. I added a few flourishes—twirling, kneeling, pretending to trip—with nary a mishap.

They applauded. My middle went soft and warm inside, like pudding. The king said, "A squire who can tumble and juggle besides! You are fortunate, Tor!"

"I am, indeed," said Tor, "though now I see I have misjudged my friend. He should not be taking care of my weapons, any lad with a strong back can do that. He should be here at court using his real talents! He is a japer par excellence."

Par excellence sounded like a compliment.

"At least in my humble opinion," added Tor.

The king's eyebrows went up and the corners of his mouth turned down. *Perhaps,* said his face.

I was astonished.

"Well, Twixt, what do you make of that idea?" Tor asked lightly.

"I would like to think about it," I replied, but I was lying. I wanted to talk it over with him.

The king dismissed us. As soon as we were out of earshot I said glumly, "I want to be a good squire."

"I know you do," said Tor. "But my weapons are very heavy. And my horse is so large that you can stand underneath him! That helps neither of you—unless you yearn to pick ticks off his belly."

I could not help smiling.

"Also," he went on, "I need my squire to ride with me. You cannot say you like riding, can you?"

I could not. Nor could I say, *You are my only friend! How can you tell me we should part?* But I was thinking it.

"All that is beside the point," said Tor. "You are an entertainer! A fine, nimble, clever one! And you can cheer the king—I saw it myself."

When I hesitated he lowered his voice. "He needs cheering, Twixt. The man has more worries than hairs in his nose. His sisters scheme against him, his nephews also. As for the queen—" He stopped abruptly.

What about the queen? I wanted to ask, but he took the conversation elsewhere. "He is the best soul in the country, you know—a great warrior, a great king . . . generous to a fault."

That was true. The first time I ever laid eyes on the king, he gave Tor an earldom. "We are all fortunate to serve him," Tor concluded.

All this time a question had been nagging at me. "I won't have to wear a costume, will I?" I hated the gaudy rags my first master had forced on me. "Or a cap with bells?"

He laughed. "You can wear what you like—the king won't care."

Now I had no excuse to say no. "Well?" asked Tor.

The words came hard. "I will do it because you think I should." *And because I owe you my life.*

He threw an arm around my shoulders. "Good man!" he cried, squeezing hard. "Excellent!"

"About his sisters?" I said when I regained my breath. "I had dealings with one of them while you were away."

He snorted. "And I am Julius Caesar's ghost!"

"It is not a jest," I said, launching into the story of how I served Morgan Le Fay. He was soon shaking his head in wonder and alarm, and when I finished he stared at me. "I am glad of your recovery *and* her departure!" he said. "May they both last forever!"

"Just thinking of it makes me daffish," I said, though it was no excuse for laughing like a dolt in the king's presence.

"So it seems," Tor said, but kindly. "Well, my friend, now you are free to play the fool to your heart's content." He lowered his voice again. "Morgan is gone for now, but that does not mean she has stopped her conniving. So keep your ears open. If you see anything suspicious, hear of anything that might threaten him, you will tell me, won't you?"

I made a solemn promise that I would.

And that is how I, once called Dungbeetle, became court jester at Camelot.

CHAPTER 25

I had been casting spells all my life, but in my time with Pelleas, I felt as if *I* had been enchanted, as if a sorcerer of endless ingenuity had decided to test his skills by finding out just how happy he could make me. *She will be happy when they speak, happy when they touch, happy when he wolfs down her cooking. She will be happy when they walk the countryside and when they swim in the Lake, happier still when they tell each other stories and rub each other's backs. They will sit at the fire admiring its colors, and this, too, will make her happy. She will forget her obligations and all prior constraints. She will live carefree, merrily breaking Rules, believing that her happy new existence will last forever.*

In this giddy state I had left all thoughts of duty behind, shrugging them off like a burdensome cloak. I forgot the Rules, and when my feet itched in remonstrance, I never worried: I rubbed them briskly with chamomile, which worked passably well. If I thought of Merlin and Nimue, I told myself that no matter what Merlin believed, he would leave his prison one day, for my cousin would repent and release him; how could she not? Then he would take up with her again, perhaps with a touch more caution. I always ended on a firmly happy note—*Merlin will rejoin Arthur; Arthur will be safe. No need to worry, no need at all.*

Instead I turned my mind to domestic magic. After conjuring up a modest little dwelling—Pelleas could not live in the Lake, as I had done—I proceeded to furnish it with chairs, a table, and a bed. Then I added the essentials: pantries that would fill themselves, moss that crept over the damp stone floors like a lazy green carpet, an ever-shifting iridescent glow for the walls, and the intoxicating fragrance of wet reeds throughout.

There was a stream that ran through our bedroom, lulling us to sleep every night, and a flock of songbirds to wake us every morning.

It was a comfortable household, dry enough for Pelleas, just wet enough for me.

Once it was running smoothly, my thoughts turned to metalwork. Our dining table needed candlesticks, preferably branchlike silver ones. Pelleas's right hand was bare—how could that be, when it cried out for a handsome gold ring? And why, I asked myself, were we using ordinary goblets when we could have gold ones, chased to look like dragon scales?

I would have to visit my smithy. As near to the house as it was, I had not been there since the making of Excalibur, in another lifetime. Not surprisingly, I found the place in sad condition.

Shamefully neglected, I thought, seeing the cobwebs, the dusty tools, the mouse droppings, *but easily fixed*. The spells for cleaning, tidying, and refurbishing—the very bedrock of domestic magic—were second nature to me now, and I cast them at once. Moments later the floor was clean, the thatch was fresh, and my tools were in pristine condition, lined up neatly on the worktable. I never worried that I was wasting magic, of course; if my feet itched, it was growing easier to ignore them. Why mind the Rules when there were so many more interesting things to do?

The gold ring first, I decided.

Making it was a lovely task but slow; it kept me away from the house for hours at a time. Pelleas never objected. He even showed an interest in what I was doing. (*Her lover delights in her every occupation!*) When, after several days, I offered the ring, he accepted it with a rush of thanks. It fit perfectly, like a coil of sunshine around his finger. Admiring it, he declared that it would never come off, ever.

"You must make a matching one for yourself," he said, and I confessed that I already had. I placed it in his hand; he slipped it onto my finger.

"There," he said, with the sweetest of smiles.

"There," I replied. We clasped hands and kissed. *If this is a wedding*, I thought, *it is the shortest one in history*. I was very happy.

Some days after we exchanged rings, Pelleas mentioned that the autumn tourneys were approaching, that he intended to fight as my champion. This yearly gathering drew knights from everywhere in Arthur's kingdom. They competed in many events—javelin tossing, archery, mounted obstacle races—but the high point of the tourney, and the most dangerous contest by far, was the joust. Knights rode at each other from opposite ends of a track, wielding their lances, and the one who unseated his opponent was the winner. The lances were blunt, but there were always injuries. By the final joust, only the two best fighters remained. According to Pelleas, Lancelot, the queen's champion, was invariably one of them.

A look of special meaning passed between us. Not so long ago Pelleas had fought for Ettard, hoping to win her esteem. He had done well, but not well enough, and his only prize was her contempt.

This year will be different, I thought.

"This year," he said, "the man to beat is Lancelot, as usual. You will come to cheer me on, won't you?"

"Of course," I said, but that night I lay awake, beset by worry. *Pelleas could be hurt so easily, so grievously! He could even be killed!* That thought was so awful that I gasped, and Pelleas, who could sleep through any wild disturbance, reached out to touch me.

I patted his hand. He sank back into sleep while I lay there, thinking.

⁂

When I went to my smithy the next morning, I did not know exactly what I would make, only that it must keep Pelleas safe without hindering his movement. The padded leather armor he wore—that most knights wore—would not hold up against

Lancelot's considerable force, and I meant to devise a garment that was just as flexible as leather, no heavier, and much, much tougher.

But what material to use?

It was an interesting puzzle, and I was convinced that the answer lay somewhere in nature. I sat on my bench for hours, pondering the ways that birds, animals, and plants defended themselves. I pictured plants with spines, thorns, and stinging poison, birds that mobbed together to repel attackers, and rodents that simply ran from harm, like mice and chipmunks. None of it obtained.

Then there were the creatures that used visual trickery: insects that passed for twigs, salamanders that changed color to match their surroundings, tadpoles that became almost invisible when they hung in the water motionless.

I got up and walked around. Snails, turtles, cockles, and mussels took refuge in their shells. Gophers, moles, and voles ran to their burrows for safety. Little fish swam away from big ones, and if they were lucky, they escaped fishing nets, too—though some nets, I reflected, were so fine that they would trap very small fish. . . .

I stopped pacing. There was something about fishing nets; what was it? A full net would hold hundreds of fish, all struggling to get out. Some fish were quite large, but the nets held, because they were woven. I sat down again, knowing I was close.

If I made something knotted or woven, I reasoned, it would be strong, and it would move easily. But I couldn't use rope, or cotton, or leather—the material had to be tougher.

Wood? I pictured Pelleas wearing a miniature fence. No.

Metal? A metal net? No.

I turned the ring on my finger absently.

Wait! Metal rings! Metal rings linked together, like a net!

Yes!

Light, strong metal links would keep my beloved safe. I was so pleased with my solution that I jumped into the Lake.

CHAPTER 26

In the end it took six days. The work was endlessly repetitive, requiring me to cast the linking spell over and over and over. (The spell was a minor one, so I wasn't really wasting magic— or that is what I chose to believe.) As the metal garment came together in my hands, I thought often of how very striking it would look on Pelleas, and this almost always led me to long, uplifting meditations on his charm and beauty.

One day when the tunic was nearly finished, I thought of Arthur. That was a surprise. At some point after saving Pelleas, I had managed to convince myself that eventually Merlin would free himself (with or without Nimue's help); and that until he did, Guinevere's love, the admiration of his court, even the fierce devotion of his jester, Twixt, would keep the king safe. In this way I had put Arthur out of my mind.

How long ago was that? I wondered, for my sense of time had grown blurry. *Two years? Three?*

Then, unbidden, a vision of Merlin came to me. He was in a dark stone chamber, his head resting on his knees, his long white hair obscuring his face. He was curled in on himself like a larva.

Rattled, I put down my work. Merlin had good reason to be sad—Nimue had betrayed him cruelly. But seeing him now, I feared there was another reason for his profound gloom, one that concerned Arthur. Suddenly the questions I had been avoiding for so long came back to me: Was Arthur safe? And if he was in danger, would I even be aware?

I did not know. I had come so far from my promises to Merlin that I might never have made them. *Willful ignorance,* I thought, *worthy of Nimue. If she were here, she would mock me. And she would be justified.*

My throat dry, I stared at the shining links on my table. Merlin, foreseeing Arthur's destiny, had put him on the throne, then guided him through years of strife to a hard-won peace. Had he known his own destiny as well, that heartbreak and betrayal were lying in wait for him like twin assassins?

I had never envied Merlin's prophetic gifts. My own—limited as they were—brought as much distress as joy. I could not bear to know that my efforts to safeguard Pelleas would fail or that despite my best intentions, an enemy would harm the king. I would rather remain ignorant.

A Lady Always Keeps Her Promises.

The skin between my toes burned as if I had stepped into an adder's nest.

I went back to work.

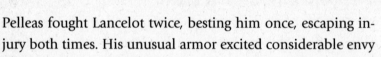

Pelleas fought Lancelot twice, besting him once, escaping injury both times. His unusual armor excited considerable envy in the tiltyard. Lancelot, Gawaine, and Pellinore led the headlong rush to have it copied, and all three were wearing reasonable facsimiles before the year's end.

"None as good as yours," Pelleas maintained. He had sworn to keep its provenance a secret, and he did; it would never occur to him to break his word.

CHAPTER 27

Pelleas never spoke ill of the king and queen or gossiped about them (for in addition to his other sterling qualities he was loyal and discreet), so I did not hear of the troubles at court until they were well and truly seething.

One spring evening, he brought the shocking news that Guinevere had been accused of treason. A young knight called Sir Patrise had succumbed to poison at a banquet two nights before, and some of the guests, led by Patrise's uncle, Sir Mador de la Porte, held Guinevere responsible.

"But why?" I asked.

"Because she was the hostess," he said. "What nonsense!" After a pause he added, "I fear for her." It was an unsettling admission; Pelleas was not a fearful man.

"Where is the king?"

"Away in Ireland with King Anguish. He should not have

gone . . . would not have gone had he known—" He broke off, frowning, and his hand went to his chest. He grimaced slightly, then wiped his forehead.

"Known what?"

"She is not well liked." Guinevere and Lancelot, he told me, had formed a close attachment whose nature was apparent to all but Arthur. Those who were aware of it (and there were many) hated the queen on her husband's account.

Dainty young Guinevere an adulteress? "No," I protested, remembering how she had hurried to the king's side, taken his arm and clung to it, how they had walked in step with such obvious contentment. "She loves Arthur."

"She loves Lancelot, too," said Pelleas, as if he had long struggled to accept the fact. "So does the king."

"And Lancelot?" I asked. "What of him?"

"He? He loves them both."

Three people whose love for one another is unevenly apportioned! I thought. *There's a human dilemma for you!* Love in the spirit world was different. It could be ardent, even passionate, but more often it was fleeting, free of jealousy and guilt. As the saying went, "The torments of love are for mortals."

Merlin might not agree, I thought.

"It is an ugly situation," said Pelleas. His face was pale, almost waxy, and I wondered if the turtle stew had disagreed with him. "Mador de la Porte is calling for her arrest."

"Lancelot is her champion. Surely he will protect her?" Pelleas was silent. "Won't he?"

"She banished him to Joyous Gard," said Pelleas, referring to Lancelot's castle, "hoping to quell the rumors. And now, with the danger growing, she is too proud to summon him back. At least that is what I have heard. . . ."

"Then she is behaving like a fool," I snapped, irked by his concern for Guinevere.

"I thought perhaps you might help her."

"Help her? How?"

Pelleas was silent. Seeing beads of sweat on his brow, I wondered again about the stew. When he winced, gripping his right arm with his left hand, I finally understood that Guinevere was not the chief cause of his distress. Something was very wrong with him.

I jumped out of my chair. "Pelleas! What ails you?" He shook his head as if to say he didn't know and fell against me with a groan. I threw my arm around him; his tunic was damp. By now I was thoroughly frightened. Kneeling so I could look up at him, I asked, "Can you speak?"

He shook his head again and I saw an unfamiliar expression on his face, one that I slowly recognized as fear. Tears sprang to my eyes. "I'm going to help you to bed," I told him, keeping my voice steady. "When you lie down, you'll feel better."

"My arm," he said tightly, "my right one, and my gut . . ."

"We've got to get you to the bed," I whispered, hauling him to his feet. "Lean on me." He was shivering now, giving off a scent like brackish water. Bearing his weight as best I could, we lurched our way to the bedchamber, where I covered him with every blanket I could find. *Healing spells! I need strong ones!* I thought frantically. I had known many before Pelleas, but now . . .

"About the queen—" he gasped, his lips tinged with blue.

The queen? I was too surprised to speak. That he was worrying about her now astonished me. It made me admire him and envy him, too. *You are such a good soul!* I thought, stroking his brow. *So steadfast! I wish I had half your virtue! Even a crumb of it!*

"I will help her," I said, taking his hand, "but first I must know who was at the banquet." *I will seek them out and search their very souls.* "Tell me if you can."

"Gawaine. Agrivaine. Gareth. Gaheris." He spoke with effort, pausing after each name. "Brandiles. Kay le Seneschal. Ector, Persant, Pinel le Savage. Mador." He went on, and when he came to the end of a long list of guests, he closed his eyes. "There," he murmured, with a long sigh.

"Sleep now," I said, unwilling to move until his chest was rising and falling steadily. Then I sank down beside him, curled up, and shut my eyes tight. With dread flapping inside me like a terrified bird, I thought, *Merlin.*

❧

"Why have you come?" His voice was weary and bitter, reminding me of two good reasons why I should not be here: I was not my cousin Nimue, and, though love had led me astray, I was still free. He had no reason to welcome me.

"Pelleas has fallen ill," I blurted. "I cannot cure him. I—I can't summon the magic! I'm afraid he'll die." I tried not to sound desperate and failed. "Merlin, tell me what to do. Please."

"Pelleas the knight?"

"Yes."

"You've fallen in love with him?"

"Yes. We've married."

"Married! Unusual for a Lady and a mortal . . ."

"We love each other." The instant the words left my mouth I regretted them. If Merlin had not been thinking of Nimue, he was now. I felt very clumsy.

"Have you been protecting Arthur?" he asked sharply.

"As—as well as I can," I stammered. I was a poor liar.

After a long silence, he said, "Make Pelleas comfortable. Prepare for the worst."

I felt a heavy, prickling sensation that scuttled up my arms and legs like an army of spiders. I had never felt such terror, and I was certain that if I did not speak at once, I would lose the power of speech altogether. "Is . . . is there nothing that can make him well?" I pleaded.

There was another silence, longer than the first. "Dark times are upon us, Damosel. You will need all your resources—for Pelleas, and for what comes after."

"What comes after?" The words were ominous enough to make me tremble. "What—?"

"However bleak the outcome," he continued, "do not give up hope. There is a beginning in every ending, remember that."

"Merlin, I don't understand!"

"No matter."

I am sorry. I am sorry. I am sorry, I thought, reeling.

"Enough," he said, as if he had heard me. "Now go."

CHAPTER 28

I never liked Mordred. In his cunning and mean spirit he was much like Esus, that swine, but cleverer. He was the king's nephew, a young man of the court who came and went as he pleased. He wore fine clothing, he dressed his hair with bergamot. I was a jester, far beneath his notice.

"I do not mind being too lowly for him," I told Sir Tor, who was hobbling alongside me with a broken leg on this fine, sunny morning. One of the new horses had thrown him, but if he was in pain he gave no sign. His concern was for the horse. We were on our way to the stables so he could check on the beast.

Tor nodded. He disliked Mordred also. ("Sweetness itself with the king but beats his horses *and* his women. About as trustworthy as his dear aunt Morgan Le Fay.")

"The less he takes note of me the better," I said. Mordred

needed watching, we both thought so, and that would be easier for me than Tor. It was not only because of my size. Many took it for granted that I was dim. They spoke freely around me, revealing secrets they would otherwise hide. And Tor was often away, finding horses for the king. He was a good judge of them.

"Coming in?" he asked mildly when we reached the stable. I agreed with Tor in most things, but I did not share his affection for the smell of horse manure, which he often compared to perfume. He knew this very well.

"Another day," I said.

That very week Sir Patrise died of poisoning and the queen was charged with treason. It smacked of mischief to me, but if Mordred was behind it, there was no proof. He was visiting his mother, Margause, at the time.

The king, just back from Ireland, was most unhappy with this turn of events. Following the law of the land, he called for a champion to fight for the queen against Patrise's uncle, Sir Mador de la Porte. If the queen's champion won, her name would be cleared. If not, she would be put to death. If no champion came forward, her fate was in the hands of Sir Mador de la Porte, and he was not a forgiving man. That was the law, harsh and clear, and the king was bound to uphold it.

In the grim days that followed, Sir Tor complained often, for with his bad leg he could not fight, and of all the other knights not a single one stepped forward. Mordred, forever trumpeting his love for the king and queen, never showed his face.

The days went by, it seemed as if the entire court was holding its breath. Then one morning a masked knight rode onto the tourney course. He said he was there for the queen, ready to fight on her behalf. "Whoever would oppose me," he challenged, "let him come!" When she heard of it the queen swooned, her face pale as a parsnip.

It was not much of a contest, the masked knight made short work of Mador de la Porte. With her rescue, the queen's spirits improved at once. When Sir Lancelot pulled off his mask, both she and the king cried out with joy. Who was happier I could not say.

I was happy, too, until I saw Mordred, standing apart with a friend. *When did you come back,* I wondered with deep burning dislike, *and why?* Looking sideways at the queen he whispered something to his companion. It could not have been praise for they both sneered. I mistrusted him more than ever. *Did your aunt Morgan Le Fay help you with her wicked magic?* I wondered, thinking it could very well be so.

But the next day the Lady of the Lake appeared before the king and queen, saying that Sir Pinel had brought the poisoned apple to the banquet, that it was meant for Sir Gawaine but Sir Patrise ate it instead. Pinel was thwarted, the queen's life endangered. "The whole affair springs from an old blood feud," said the Lady. "It is festering even now." There was no mistaking how she felt about such goings-on. When I first saw her she was gentle and timid, now she was bolder but sorrowful, too. Our eyes met and she smiled very kindly, then she melted away.

No matter what the Lady said, my suspicions of Mordred remained. In fact he was guilty of much worse than poisoning an apple, but that came later.

For the present Lancelot was at court, and he and the royal couple were often together, leaving me free to do my spying. Here my size was always a boon, easing my entry into many out-of-the-way places, the underside of Mordred's bed being one.

The first time I hid there I heard him curse Arthur bitterly. The next time he went on about the queen and Lancelot. They were in love, he muttered, they had tried to stay apart and failed. *So the rumors are true!* I thought. I never doubted him, it was just the kind of thing he would ferret out. He said their love would seal their doom and the king's, too. He would see to it himself.

I knew malevolence and its many faces, the one snarling without provocation was all too familiar. In my time at Camelot I had almost forgotten what it looked like. Now Mordred reminded me.

I wondered if I should send a message to Tor. He was gone again, even farther north this time. But what would it say? That Mordred hated Lancelot as well as the royal couple? That he dreamed of ruining them? Tor knew most of it already. I decided to wait a few days, until after the king's hunt.

I had come by many *objets de luxe* with my elevation to court jester, but the best was a pony cart with red wheels and gilded railings, a gift from the king. The queen gave me Daisy, a little gray who pulled the cart at a clip. She did not like to fall behind the other horses, she hurried against them even when they were twice her size, like the huge coursers ridden by the royal party.

Still, she was not always able to keep up. After two days' hunting with the king and a party of knights, we were the very last to reach the castle. Except for a cluster of stable boys talking quietly, the courtyard was deserted.

I jumped down to untack Daisy when Amren, looking wild-eyed, ran over to me.

"Is something amiss?" I asked. He was Severn's younger brother, steady and capable beyond his years. I had never seen him in this state. "What is it?"

"Lancelot just killed twelve knights!" he blurted.

My mouth fell open. "Why?"

"Some of the knights heard he was in the queen's chambers, so they broke in and found him there. He fought them off. He wasn't even armed!"

"Which knights?"

"Mordred, Agrivaine . . . and some others."

Hearing Mordred's name I thought, *Of course. That's why he begged off the hunt and stayed here. He had more important things to do.* "Was Mordred killed?" I asked hopefully.

"Agrivaine was, and Mador de la Porte. Also Galleron of Galway, Meliot de Logris, Astamore, Gingaline, Petipase, Melion of the Mountain, Gromore, Curselaine, Florence, and Lovel . . . but Mordred was only wounded."

I was sorry to hear about Agrivaine and the others, sorrier still that Mordred was still alive. "And Lancelot?" I asked. "Where is he now?"

"At Joyous Gard," Amren replied miserably. Lancelot was a god to the younger boys. If he did kill twelve of the king's men, he would not be safe even in his own castle. At the very least he would be banished.

Terrible, terrible, I thought, handing my reins to Amren and hurrying into the castle. I did not ask about the queen, but three of her women were sobbing in the corridor, that boded ill.

The king's privy chamber was crowded, and he in heated conversation with Gawaine, Gareth, and Gaheris, Agrivaine's brothers. Standing behind the throne was Mordred. Unlike his older siblings he was a marvel of composure. All this cruel mayhem was his dream come true, he had longed for it and likely unleashed it. Yet no pleasure shone in his eyes, no smile played on his lips. He was the very soul of grave concern.

If I did not know him, I thought, *and he told me that his only wish was to help the king, I would believe him. In a trice.*

CHAPTER 29

Mordred did not do it, he was too clever to come forward himself, but the very next day the queen was accused of adultery. She was tried at once, and the king presided, it was his duty. I think it broke his heart, for the guilty verdict made her a traitor and condemned her to death. When he heard it, he said only, "We will abide by the law."

I tried to cheer him, I juggled and danced and barked like a dog, but it was useless. Nothing would raise his spirits, they were lower than the dungeon floor, and so were mine. *Why did I put it off?* I asked myself over and over. *I should have sent word to Tor before it was too late.*

All that talk of playing the fool, as if I was ever anything else! Dunce, dunce, dunce! In this state of mind I went to bid the queen farewell on the day of her execution.

She had always laughed like a girl at my antics. Now she

was dressed in a white shift with her hair unbound, looking too young to be a queen, much less a traitor. I kissed her hand and saw that her feet were bare. *How cold they must be,* I thought. Then she, who had given me many pairs of soft leather boots, gave me her blessing, and I scurried away.

The king was alone in his privy chamber, head in hands. "I will not watch it," he said, so inside we stayed, avoiding each other's eyes until an acrid smell wafted in. It could only be smoke from the stake.

"Leave me," he said brusquely, and I fled down the corridor with the smell of smoke following. Suddenly I remembered lying in the dark in the ale cellar after running from Morgan Le Fay. *My time down there was a maypole dance compared to this,* I thought, yearning heartily to hide myself away.

But I would not, I would stay near the king in case he needed me. I turned back, noting the eerie quiet. Everyone was outside waiting.

On my way back to the privy chamber I heard a sound, deep as a drumroll. It grew louder and faster. Horses, many of them, were coming at a gallop. I hurried to a window just in time to see them ride in. There were a dozen men at least, Lancelot in front.

"Clear away!" he shouted, brandishing his sword. "Get back!" The churning crowd made haste to obey and Lancelot and his men plowed through, closer and closer to the stake. The queen had worked her hands free of her bonds, she stood on the platform with her arms outstretched like a child waiting to be lifted.

There were many knights loyal to the king in the crowd, now they massed in front of the stake to block the rescue. Some of them were not fully armed, yet they stood their ground with the others. And still Lancelot came on. I had seen him fight before but never like this. He cut down every man in his path, wielding his sword so furiously that he seemed to move in a bright red mist. Finally he was close enough to slash through the ropes around the queen's ankles. She fell into his arms. His face was bloody, hers was scorched. They kissed and rode away.

Good for them! I thought.

I would swear the king felt the same. He never wanted the queen to die or Lancelot either. When told of the rescue he exclaimed, "How did he do it?" The admiration in his voice was hard to miss.

Mordred felt otherwise, of course. He was still intent on stirring up hatred, and after the queen's escape he found an ally in Gawaine for the saddest of reasons. While fighting his way through the crowd, Lancelot killed Gawaine's younger brother Gareth. He could not have known what he was doing, he was very fond of the boy.

"Gareth worshipped him!" Gawaine told the king in an audience the next day. "Agrivaine, too, for all the good it did him!"

"We have all lost too much," said the king after a long pause.

His measured reply did not satisfy Gawaine. "He killed two of my brothers! I will have my revenge!" he spat, before turning on his heel.

"So much for his vow of mercy," said the queen when she was told of it later. And from then on Gawaine would not hear a good word about his former friend, much less utter one.

Meanwhile, the king lost all semblance of cheer, with new lines on his brow attesting to his heaviness of heart. He drank more, ate less, and withdrew to the north tower of the castle whenever he could.

I stopped spying on Mordred, for what was the point? I did not want to hear him gloating over the king's decline. He marked and savored it and doubtless would work it to some disgusting advantage.

"It rankles me so," I told Tor the morning after he returned to Camelot from the north. We were sitting near the stables in the autumn sun, and I was telling him about the queen's trial and her rescue. "I should have tried to reach you," I said, "as soon as I heard him railing against Lancelot and the queen. We might have done something to keep him at bay." The thought still hurt.

"Not likely," said Tor. "I was in spitting distance of Hadrian's Wall."

That was very far north, almost in Caledonia.

"Much too far to get here in time, even if I galloped all the way," he said. "None of this is your fault."

I felt a little better.

"How long since the queen and Lancelot went home to Joyous Gard?" he asked.

"Weeks. And his friends are joining him there. Have you heard the rumor that he is preparing to battle the king?"

"Last night," said Tor, chewing on a piece of straw. "Before I even watered my horse."

"I am certain Mordred is putting it about," I said.

"It does smack of him."

"He hopes the two will kill each other. Then he could seize the throne." I looked at Tor anxiously. "It could happen, couldn't it?"

"Yes."

I shivered. Then Tor said, "I am on good terms with Lancelot. I could speak to him."

"Will you tell the king?"

"Do you think I should? He might object."

"It's worse if you don't tell him," I said. "If you went to Joyous Gard and Mordred found out, he would be accusing you of treason in a blink."

"Shrewd," said Tor. "I'll take your advice."

He left the next day with the king's approval.

That night I lay thinking about the God of Luck and his caprices, how he could be generous one moment, indifferent the next. I was wary of asking too much of him. But it was time. I climbed out of bed, fell to my knees, and begged him to favor us.

CHAPTER 30

In the last days I shared with Pelleas, I followed Merlin's instructions as best I could. I made my beloved comfortable, sat with him day and night, and learned about his family and its afflictions. His father's father, his father, and his uncle had all died, he said, after sudden collapses like his own.

"Not one of them fell in battle," he said. "For a fighting man, dying at home is cause for shame. My father denied it, but my mother used to say it was a curse. After he died, she took to hanging talismans and charms around my neck, hoping to stave it off. She prayed for me, too." He smiled. "She was not a Christian, mind you, she simply talked a priest into teaching her the prayers. She used to say it couldn't hurt."

"And you?" I asked. "What did you think?"

"I thought the charms and prayers were useless against it,

that it was something in our blood . . . like our blue eyes or dark hair. One day I asked the healing woman and she said I might be right, she didn't know." He stroked my hand. "It may just be that dying young is a family tradition."

Seeing my tears, he said, "I should have told you. But I couldn't."

"Why?"

"You would have worried too much," he said. "I didn't want that."

Later I came to accept his decision, but at first I could only think, *You are living but a moment in my time! It could have been different! I would have protected you no matter how much magic it took!* As I wiped his brow, held his hands, helped him to drink, the reproach was there between us, lingering even when I told him I had spoken on behalf of Guinevere in the matter of Sir Patrise's poisoning.

When I brought the news that Lancelot had fought for the queen and won, Pelleas nodded, clasping my hand weakly. It was getting harder for him to speak, so I was surprised when he said, very clearly, "Damosel, you must forgive me."

The words went straight to my heart, dissolving every last trace of resentment until only love remained. "Nothing to forgive," I said, "nothing at all."

The next morning, while the birds were welcoming the day at first light, he whispered, "Bury me near the Lake."

"Are you sure?" I asked, thinking he might want his body sent home to his mother in Caerwent. He looked at me as he used to, before he was weak and stricken, the warmth in his eyes like an embrace. "Yes," he said, and in his mind I saw us walking along the shore in the bright flickering light of early spring. We were hand in hand, swinging our arms, smiling. Then the light went dark, taking us with it, and he was gone.

⁂

I buried him in his chain mail, a long, wearying task. Then I lay down on his side of the bed and buried my face in his pillow. For days after I could hear his voice and see his face, and this, along with the few possessions he had left behind—a heart-shaped rock, a knife, a wooden comb—allowed me to pretend he was still there. I knew that the presence I clung to was not really Pelleas, but I would take a wraith over nothing. What I dreaded most was the day when I forgot his scent and the sound of his voice, forgot the way he looked when we were closest, his face soft with affection, and surely that day must come, for there was no magic strong enough to keep him with me; that had already been proven.

But I could not let him go just yet, so I withdrew from the world even further, into an echoing solitude where we could be together undisturbed. I visited his grave every day, bringing hyacinths and primroses in spring, roses, marguerites, and lilies in summer. I went to my smithy but made nothing. I drifted in the Lake for hours at a time, for his image was brighter there than anywhere else.

Then, one warm afternoon, I found that I could no longer hear his voice or see him clearly. Distraught, I entered the Lake, but even there his image was muzzy and wavering. When

157

I was back on shore it occurred to me to wonder just how many years had gone by. One? Two? I didn't know.

I did know, as I looked around with newly sharpened attention, that somehow the trees had thrown off their leaves. Now—how had it happened so quickly?—their limbs were bare. We were well into autumn. That meant Samhain was approaching.

Samhain is a time when barriers between the worlds dissolve and spirits roam freely. They are easier to summon then, appearing when invited. Every year a trio of crows welcomes the day by screeching "Hurry! Hurry!" from the top of the chestnut tree, and this year was no different. Hearing them, I wondered if they were hectoring the wind, or squirrels, or ghosts. Then I realized they were cawing at me—with special vehemence, too—taking umbrage at my slowness and distraction.

So I heeded them. At sundown I stationed myself at Pelleas's grave, and when the moon appeared, I called to him.

"Damosel," he whispered, so quickly that he might have been waiting. At the sound of his voice tears sprang to my eyes. Then I could see him. He was thin and pale, his eyes deep-set and his hair unkempt, much as he had been when he died. I stretched out my hands and he took them. I felt a soft chill, as if I were touching the first snow of winter.

"I wanted so much to save you," I said, hot tears coursing down my cheeks.

"I know."

"And now you're leaving me!"

"But here I am!" He smiled teasingly, as he used to. "Yours alone."

This made me sob. I shook my head, unable to speak. He hesitated for a moment, then stepped forward, enfolding me in his arms. When I felt his body against mine, I gasped. He meant to console me, but his embrace was unendurably cold.

Shuddering, I drew away. My breath steamed in the air and we exchanged a long, rueful look. *Such beautiful eyes,* I thought.

"I love you," I told him, "and I always will, even if we never see each other again." Saying the words, I knew they were true.

"My Damosel," he said, reaching for me. I pressed my lips to his until they burned with cold, and then I let him go.

CHAPTER 31

On the day the queen came back to Camelot I whispered, "Thank you, Luck! Thank you for heeding my prayers!" After Tor made three visits to Joyous Gard, smoothing the way for her return, she was once more at the king's side. He forgave her, and she seemed content. If she missed Lancelot, who had since gone to his lands in France, she gave no sign.

Now all will be well, I thought hopefully. *The rifts in court and kingdom will heal, the dark days will end.* I was glad to see her back.

Over the next weeks they were careful with each other, she less girlish than before, he attentive and grave. There was much gossip in the kitchen about the marriage. "A child would save it," said the head cook, "a good, hard-kicking little boy."

"A proper heir is what they need," declared the kitchen gardener, sorting through the beans.

"Even a girl," said Agnes to another young scullion, and they nodded in unison over the carrots.

"Mmm," a baker murmured dubiously. Picturing a little rosy-cheeked Guinevere with amber curls, I thought, *I could care for her. I could take her for rides in my cart!*

And if anybody should have a family of their own, it was the king and queen. His relations were a thoroughly bad bunch, highborn and low-minded. The very thought of Morgan Le Fay made my throat close up, Margause and her sons Gawaine and Gaheris hated Arthur almost as much as Morgan did, and I knew Mordred's feelings all too well.

A boy or a girl, I prayed, *either one. Just give them a child.*

Alas, Luck frowned on Arthur and scowled at Guinevere, for no child came. The queen took to prayer and embroidery. The king busied himself with his borders, riding north or east at any hint of a Saxon threat. The country was secure, but he must keep it so, was what he said. Mordred encouraged him, contriving to remain at court during the king's many forays.

I knew Mordred's nature, I suspected the worst of him, yet once again he made a fool of me.

It fell out this way: After Lancelot went to France, Mordred set about to blacken his name. He maligned that brave knight at every opportunity, and Gawaine was more than happy to chime in. Lancelot was a threat, they said, he was surely amassing an army in France, stop him now, Majesty, attack him before he strikes! They went on and on in this fashion, I wished I had a spell to shut them up.

All the while Guinevere listened with her eyes lowered. Regret, longing, who could tell what was hidden there? She said nothing. With Merlin long out of sight and the Lady of the Lake keeping her distance, the king lacked good counsel when he needed it most.

Like the queen, I said nothing to the king. He was not in the habit of asking my advice and it was not my place to offer it. And what could I say if he did ask? That Mordred hated him and schemed against him? That a war with Lancelot was folly, and only Mordred would find a way to benefit? I had no proof, it would be my word against his, and Mordred was a brilliant liar. If there was a tourney for liars, he would win.

One day not long after Lancelot's departure two men appeared at court saying they were from Calais, a town across the Narrow Sea. They swore that Lancelot meant to unseat the king, they had been hearing it up and down the coast.

"When?" asked Mordred with no sign of emotion.

"When his army is big enough."

"How far off is that?" demanded Gawaine, nearly slavering with eagerness.

The two men conversed rapidly. "Less than a fortnight," said one.

"Less than ten days," said the other, after a quick uncertain glance at Mordred. *Why look at him?* I wondered. The answer was hovering nearby, almost within reach, but I never grasped it until later. By then it was useless.

Meanwhile Gawaine was pushing for a quick strike. "Let's surprise him!" he urged, even as the king hung back. *He does not want to fight Lancelot,* I thought. *Despite everything, he loves the man.*

But when the king wavered and turned to Mordred I knew what would happen, and it did: Mordred agreed with Gawaine, and five days later the king was leading an army to France. Gawaine, full of bitter purpose, rode at his right hand.

And Mordred? He stayed behind as the king's regent.

That frightened me. Being left at Camelot with Mordred in charge was like being locked in an attic with a rabid bat. But when I asked the king if I could please come with him to France, he smiled. "Stop your jesting!" he said, though I was never more in earnest. "You must stay here and take care of the queen."

So that is what I did.

CHAPTER 32

I felt no desolation, only a dull flatness of spirit. Now that my struggle to keep Pelleas alive was over, I found myself exhausted, inclined to do nothing but stay in the house we had shared. Day after day I sat at the window looking out at the Lake. A pair of swans had come, and I watched them for hours on end. They glided majestically from one side of the Lake to the other with their eyes straight ahead, as if making a royal passage. Every so often one of them would up-end itself abruptly, so that only its round white bottom showed above the water's surface. They took turns at this and it never failed to make me smile, though when they shared their findings, passing some hapless wriggling thing between them, I would feel a twinge like pain. It always faded quickly, though.

Eventually the days grew so dark and short that they were no more than brief intervals between one night and the next. The ground froze. Snow fell. I moved to the hearth and the fire became my companion, dancing tirelessly to the hiss and crackle of burning wood. I watched and listened and did little else.

Then one day as I sat at the fire, the skin between my toes began to itch ferociously and an entire set of Rules—the ones regarding Vows and Promises—popped into my head. It was a rude shock. Had I once enjoyed knowing these? Now they were like unwelcome acquaintances demanding attention. Clamoring loudest were *The Rule of Soberly Made Promises, The Rule of Scrupulously Kept Promises,* and *The Rule of Eternally Binding Vows to Wielders of Magic, Especially Wizards.*

I blinked in dismay. I had made a binding vow to the great wizard Merlin himself and then broken it. I had not watched over Arthur with anything resembling vigilance, as I had promised; in fact, after meeting Pelleas, I had hardly thought of the king at all. Had Arthur needed my help? I truly didn't know. Disgraceful.

I began pacing between the hearth and the window. There were penalties for rule-breaking, and now they came back to me. Some were mild (Itching and Burning), some severe (Temporary Loss of Powers), and some shudder-inducing (Permanent Loss of Powers, Double-Digit Life Span). It was true that I had itched and burned while living with Pelleas, and that I had ignored the discomfort every time. But I had not lost my powers. Everything around me—the damp, glistening walls, the moss-strewn floor, the polished candlesticks on the table, the lovely scent of wet reeds in the air—attested to that. All was in perfect order, as it should be.

Domestic magic is for beginners, said a bright, mocking interior voice that reminded me of Nimue. *Is that all you can do?* Well, no, I told it, I had summoned Pelleas. Calling up a ghost, even on Samhain, was far beyond beginner's magic.

And why is Pelleas a ghost? taunted the voice. *Shouldn't he be alive and in his prime? He died because you failed him.*

To that I had no answer.

The next morning I woke in a state of keen agitation, with a long list of Rules in my head. I remembered more while I rose, dressed, and walked outside into the morning sunshine (how bright it was!), more again as I chewed a withered apple and began to circle the Lake. I went slowly, whispering the Rules as they came to me. It was like remembering directions or the words to a song, but these directions could have guided me all the way to Avalon, and the words belonged to a song that would take a week to sing.

I never questioned the how or the why of it. Merlin had said, "Prepare for the worst," and if reacquainting myself with each and every one of *The Rules Governing the Ladies of the Lake* was preparation, so be it.

Day One
Rules of Domestic Magic (Cooking, Cleaning, Furnishings & Their Suitability, Fragrance & Its Uses). I ordered the bedclothes to change themselves and enhanced the aroma of reeds in the house with a hint of ripe seaweed.

Day Two

Rules of Obligation & Duty, Including Those Concerning the Frittering Away of Magic; Rules of Courtesy, 1 (Fairies, Gnomes, Goblins, Hobs, Imps, Nixies, Pixies, Sprites, Trolls); Rules of Courtesy, 2 (Royalty, Children, Creatures of the Wild, All Others). After burning with shame until dusk, I exchanged pleasantries with the swans and discussed the weather with an owl.

Day Three

Rules of Dress; Rules of Grooming (Wet & Dry); Rules of Comportment; Rules of Glamour. I examined my reflection in the Lake. It was appalling. My gown was filthy and so was my hair, which had gone from greenish gold to the color of mud. My face was as sallow as a bullfrog's rump, and my eyes, normally a pleasant yellowy green, were small, red, and wary.

This will not do at all, I thought. *You look worse than a water vole.* I bathed, washed my hair, and arranged it into the requisite eighty-six plaits. Then I oiled my feet, trimmed the claws that had once been toenails, and put on a clean gown.

Day Four

Numerical Rules; Rules of Transmogrification; Rules of Combat & Contest. In the morning I changed

myself into a mist, a fog, and a low-lying cloud.
In the afternoon I stared down a falcon.

Day Five
*Rules of Suasion, Thrall & Pixilation, Including
Benedictions, Rhythmic Love Chants, Hypnotic
Gestures & Captivating Footwork.* I sent a long
blessing to Merlin, hoping it would ease his
pain. Then I coaxed a water lily into bloom.

Day Six
*Rules of Thwarting & Repulsing, Including Curses,
Maledictions & Painfully Wounding Remarks.* I
attempted a spell that would curse Nimue with a
rigorous conscience. If it succeeded, she would
carry a heavy burden of regret for a long, long
time.

Day Seven
*Rules of Regeneration & Healing; Rules of Prophecy,
Including Visions, Apparitions & Incomprehensible
Sightings.* The healing Rules reminded me that
Pelleas was gone, never to return. After a burst of
self-pity I thought, *I can still help Arthur if he
needs help,* and then I was in the Lake, facedown,
waiting to find out if he did.

CHAPTER 33

Luck ignored my prayers. If he smiled on anyone, it was Mordred, and that was hard cheese to swallow. In my humble opinion the king should have banished him, not made him regent. But that was Luck for you: now Mordred was on the throne, powerful and safe, while the king and hundreds of loyal men risked their lives for no good reason. Why chase Lancelot now that Guinevere was back? The king should have stayed here with her.

But he was gone, and in his absence my only consolation was her company. She made me feel as welcome as any of her ladies, and I soon found myself visiting her every day. I would come in late morning to sit and talk with her while she embroidered. Her stitches were small and precise, the red dragon appearing on the king's tunic slowly but surely. The first tunic she made was battle-worn and this would replace it. The sign of the Pendragons was much more work than a cross, she said with the hint of a smile.

She herself prayed twice a day in a little closet off her bedchamber. One day when I came at the usual hour I was told she was still at prayer. Lady Bronwyn motioned me in, closing the outer door firmly behind me. "Wait here," she said. "She will come soon."

It was unusual for the queen to be praying so late. And Lady Bronwyn looked nothing like her usual placid self. Her face was pinched and mottled.

"Something is amiss?" I asked.

The lady sighed. She was older than the queen, a small, fair-haired woman with a soft manner. "She will tell you," she said, leaving me alone. There was nothing to do but sit with the kittens, Cinder and Dodie. They scampered up and down my chest, light and fluffy as chicks, but clawed like stilettos.

"Ow! You are dangerous little devils," I scolded. With that the queen and Lady Bronwyn appeared. The queen's face was splotchy, her eyes red.

"Twixt! I am glad to see you," she cried. "Come sit with me." She dropped into her favorite chair and I took the footstool. She blew her nose, dabbed at her teary eyes, and shook her head. All the while she could not speak.

Why is she so shaken? I wondered. *She was calmer when she was waiting to be burned at the stake.* An awful thought came to me. "Is it bad news about the king?"

She shook her head again. "It is Mordred."

"What has he done?"

"He wants to marry me."

"What!?" At my shout Dodie squeaked and ran. "How—how can he even think such a thing?" I sputtered.

"He has been regent now for how many weeks?" she replied. "Three? Four?"

I did a quick calculation. "If that."

"Well, that is long enough for him, it seems. He wants more. The throne, to be exact."

Of course, I thought. Here were my worst suspicions about Mordred confirmed.

"He claims that nothing will stand in his way, that he has all the support he needs. Can he be right? Have all the men loyal to Arthur gone with him?"

I did not like to say Mordred was right about anything, but here I was forced to. The men who stayed behind were his. They followed him around like a mangy, ill-tempered pack. *Curs every one*, I thought.

"Do you know what he said to me?" she asked.

"No."

"He said our marriage would 'fortify his position'! As if that would sway me!" She fell back in her chair, her eyes closed. "Oh God, the gall of the man. I cannot believe it!"

I can, I thought. *He planned it. He kept his men behind, he waited for the king to sail away, and then he made his move.* It was very much like him, slimy but clever.

Well, I can be clever too—sometimes. I took a deep breath. "When did you last speak with him?" I asked the queen.

"This morning."

"And what did you say?"

"I said I was surprised. He assured me I would get used to

the idea. He is loathsome! And young enough to be my son!" She made a most unqueenly noise of disgust.

"*Loathsome* is too kind a word for him," I said. Words like *loathsome* and *heinous* and *disgusting* always called Esus and Borvo to mind. My ignorance and fear helped them capture me, but the queen was not ignorant. She was not afraid, either, only angry.

"You must outwit him—stall for time so you can get away," I said, wondering if she had it in her to outwit sly Mordred. *She lied to the king and he is no fool*, I thought.

She broke into fresh tears, shaking her head no. "I do not want to be deceitful," she sobbed. "I swore to Arthur—and to myself—that I would never lie again, after . . ." Her eyes fell.

After Lancelot, I thought. *Well, too bad.* "This will be the last time, but you must," I told her. *Besides*, I thought, *I made a promise to him, too. I promised I would take care of you.* A plan was coming to me, and I spoke firmly.

"Are the men in Londinium loyal to the king?" I asked. Tor told me once that Arthur's soldiers lived in the old Roman barracks in the city. Its fortress towers were built to last forever, he said, they were three feet thick. If the queen took refuge there she would be safe from Mordred—for a time, anyway. Meanwhile, a message would be on its way to France.

Now the Lady Bronwyn spoke up. "My nephews Piers and Persant are stationed in Londinium," she said. "I can send word to them. They will help in any way they can; I know that. They are fine boys, very loyal."

"Good," I said. "The sooner the better. There is no time to spare."

"But why would I be going?" asked the queen, still forlorn. "I have no business in Londinium."

"You might," I said. "If you tell Mordred you will marry him—"

"No!" Her face went white.

"—and that you want a grand royal wedding and a splendid feast . . ."

Lady Bronwyn was quick to catch my drift. "Ah," she said, her eyes shining. "Such a wedding requires *much* preparation. The queen will wish to visit Londinium to purchase goods for it. Silk and velvet for gowns . . ."

I nodded to encourage her.

"Fine linens for the tables . . ."

"Oh yes, now I see!" cried the queen, sitting up straight for the first time. "I will need bolts and bolts of everything! I must call on the silversmiths of Silver Street, too, for silver!"

"And the Gallic wine merchants," said the Lady Bronwyn.

"What about musicians?" I prompted.

"I will have to hear them all!" said the queen. "The Pictish pipers, the Jute lutenists, the horn players of Blatfordshire— such a wedding must have only the best!" She turned her gaze heavenward, clasping her hands as if in prayer. Then she smiled at us with some of her old high spirits, it made her beautiful again. "I hope—no, I *think* he will believe it," she said.

"I think you will make him believe it," said I.

So now I was the general of an army of three. Planning our desperate campaign was like juggling. Every piece must be kept in balance, the timing never less than perfect. I was in a cold sweat for three days, knowing how easily something could go wrong—the queen failing to convince Mordred, the messages to Londinium lost or intercepted, a loose word rolling into the wrong ear.

I have never said so many heartfelt prayers to Luck. And in the end he must have heard me, for all went well.

The queen did herself proud with Mordred. "May God forgive me," she said when their interview was over, "I have never lied so hard in my life." Then she slept all day and all night.

The upshot was that Mordred gave her leave to go and ample coinage for her purchases. Picturing his face when he learned what he had paid for—bribes, food, lodging, and nary a whisper of silk—cheered me to my toes.

With our escape funded, we waited anxiously to hear from the abbess of Our Lady of the Sorrows. The queen had sent her a message about the true nature of our journey, requesting shelter at the convent. After a night there, we would continue on to Londinium, another day's ride.

The abbess was an old friend of the queen's mother, which Mordred did not know. She responded at once, inviting our party to stay as long as we liked. Mordred was not a Christian, at least not yet, but her reply had the desired effect. He asked no more questions about the journey.

Then Lady Bronwyn had word from her nephews. They would proudly safeguard the queen in the city. *On with the campaign!* I thought, and we quickly finished our preparations. The ladies Nortrude and Martha, both discreet and nimble-witted, joined us. So did Severn the groom and Agnes the scullion.

The queen packed her jewelry. Horses, carriages, and provisions were assembled, calm farewells were said.

Then off we went.

PART FIVE

In Which Damosel Rejoins the King

When I first entered the Lake, seeking a vision of Arthur, I hoped that I would see him safely at Camelot, busy with the mundane affairs of court. I floated and my mind cleared slowly, bits of internal chatter settling like tea leaves at the bottom of a cup. Eventually I was free of hopes and wishes and simply went where the water took me.

I do not know how much time passed, only that when the vision came, it was unclear. I was looking down at a field from high above, aware that the Lake and the sea were nearby. I descended, and the jumble of shapes and colors beneath me suddenly sharpened, until I was seeing the aftermath of a battle in merciless detail. Corpses lay thick on the ground, mangled, bloody, as if they had been torn apart and flung. Some faces were twisted in rage or horror. Others looked oddly peaceful, as if severed limbs, broken swords, and gouts of blood were nothing more than features of the landscape. A flock of crows was starting to spiral down.

Then I saw Arthur. He was at the very edge of the field, scarcely a mile from the southern shore of the Lake, propped in the arms of a soldier. Excalibur was at his side, and he took hold of the sword, as if to give it to the soldier. But the effort was too much for him, and he sank back. There was a rag, a makeshift bandage, on his temple, and now it fell away, revealing a long, open wound. The soldier replaced it, Arthur spoke, and the soldier shook his head in refusal.

They argued. Arthur was weak and bleeding heavily, but he prevailed, for after a moment the soldier laid him on the ground, took Excalibur, and trudged off toward the Lake. With this, Arthur closed his eyes and the vision faded.

My eyes flew open.

I was in the Lake. It was afternoon. I had just seen Arthur, badly wounded, and he had given away Excalibur. *No!* I thought, fully awake now and hurrying to shore. *It is too soon!*

Years ago, soon after Arthur became king, I gave him Excalibur, the sword I had made for him at Merlin's request. Arthur had agreed to return it to the Lake when he no longer needed it. But that day was far off—it would be countless years before he fought his last battle, or so we believed at the time.

And now, it seemed, that day had come. *Too soon!* I thought again, knowing it was useless to protest.

Some things cannot be changed.

I saw a flash of light in the faultless blue sky, brilliant and fiery as a falling star. I transported myself back to the center of the Lake and raised my arm.

Excalibur came down, end over end over end, into my waiting hand, and then I went to Arthur.

CHAPTER 35

Three of Mordred's men joined us when we left the castle—for our safety, they claimed. They were rough and shifty-eyed and could only be spies. So we were careful of what we said. Feigning cheer while feeling otherwise was not beyond the queen or me, by this time we were old hands. Besides, these men were not the sharpest axes in the armory.

We took the Roman road, a broad one passing many settlements and holdings. For most of the way the land was flat, with long views of fields and green countryside edged with forest. Then, on the third day, a ring of stones came up on the horizon. I had heard of this place, it was a temple to the old gods, built by Merlin and still in use. Giants' Dance, the Henge, and Solstice Gate were a few of its names.

The stones loomed over the plain like waiting giants. Big things and some big people had a way of making me feel even smaller than I was, but the closer we came to the stones, the more I liked them. Mayhap they were lucky, that would explain their attraction. I felt the draw in my middle, unsettling but pleasant, it made me hope we would linger.

The queen was not of like mind, however. She crossed herself as we approached, her ladies following suit. Mordred's men, too, were inclined to hurry, the cowardly sots hardly dared look at it. Only Severn and Agnes, whispering together, seemed to feel as I did. Nevertheless, we were not majesty, much less brute force. There would be no stopping. We moved on apace.

The rest of the journey passed quickly enough, the road becoming busier every day. I drew many curious glances and returned a few. I was bolder now, with my new station in life I could hold my head up. To travel with the queen was a great honor, to help her at the king's behest doubly so. If Esus and Borvo could see me they would keel over dead with their eyes popping out. Thinking it warmed my heart all the way to the convent.

We reached it after nightfall on the fifth day. Inside its walls we found a good-sized stone building, unadorned but for a large cross. Other, smaller buildings lay beyond. I spied a kitchen garden and some pasturage, too. All was orderly and clean, yet welcoming. The abbess came out to greet us, doing so with great courtesy and restraint, the queen responding in kind. She dismissed Mordred's men after giving them a message for her so-called betrothed. We would be away longer than planned, she said, perhaps more than a fortnight, for there was more to do in Londinium than we thought. She had them repeat the message, then watched calmly as they galloped away.

As soon as the men were out of sight, the queen and the

abbess embraced with great affection. Then all the women cried. After that they laughed, and then they went to supper in the dining hall. The men, otherwise known as Severn and me, were taken to the kitchen. Here three cooks, all nuns, worked busily without exchanging a word. One motioned to us to sit by the hearth, another gave us bread, pottage, apples, and ale. Everything tasted very good, but I was almost too tired to chew. While we ate, nuns passed in and out, carrying trays and bowls. By the time these were washed and the floor swept, bells were chiming. All the sisters left, the last one pausing in the doorway.

"Compline," she said. "Evening prayers."

Prayers? I thought, yearning deeply for bed. *For the queen, yes, but not for me!* The nun's face was long and thin, her eyes sharp. There was no telling her age, she might have been fifteen or thirty. Young or old, she had the look of someone who brooked no refusal. Severn got up obediently and after a moment so did I, yawning so hard my jaw cracked.

There were forty nuns or so in the chapel, kneeling in rows. Their faces were radiant, the light golden. When they chanted, the candles on the altar seemed to flicker in time. It was very soothing. We sat at the back with our heads bowed and our hands together.

"Never seen so many women in one place," Severn whispered out of the side of his mouth, "and I have eight sisters."

I knew enough not to laugh aloud. Anyway, I was too tired. The nuns continued their chanting, its soft, echoing murmur a welcome invitation to rest. I leaned my head on my hands and closed my eyes. After a moment my head jerked up. I was falling asleep. *Ah well*, I thought, *I hope I don't snore.*

CHAPTER 36

I woke on a straw pallet in a room full of sacks and jars, the kitchen pantry from the looks of it. There was a line of daylight showing under the door, but no sign of Severn. He must have carried me in last night and slept here too—I smelled horse.

My stomach growled. Why didn't he wake me earlier? We were meant to start at dawn. Londinium was just across the river, and the Lady Bronwyn's nephews waited.

I opened the door and was pleased to find myself in the kitchen, alone but for a large cheese and many loaves of bread. It was a rare chance to eat my fill, and I did so eagerly, never stopping to wonder where the cooks had gone.

My belly full, I set off in search of Severn. The back door of the kitchen led to the garden, its long, neat furrows waiting to be sown. Through the garden gate, past the well, and there were the horses and my Daisy, groomed and bridled for the day's journey. *Still no Severn,* I thought, and that very moment the convent bells began to toll. They made a harsh, urgent sound, nothing like the slow, deliberate pealing that marked the hours. No. More like an alarm.

I ran back in through the kitchen, my mind whirring. Had Mordred's men found us out and come back? I doubted it. They believed everything the queen told them. By now they would be skulking past the Henge.

Then what was it?

In the hallway nuns were running pell-mell, holding up their skirts to keep from tripping. Their bare ankles were as white as wimples. When the bell stopped, the hallways echoed with the slapping of their shoes. I followed them to the chapel and found it full to bursting with nuns and country folk. Some children rode high above the crowd on tall shoulders, seeing what I could not. I strained my ears and heard fear and confusion, much like what I felt.

The throng of big bodies was a wall, I would have to push my way through. A shove here, a tap there, many sharp tugs on black skirts, and I was a little closer to the altar.

A handbell chimed. The commotion stopped and so did I.

"Good morning, my children," a woman said, likely the abbess. "We have just received a message, a sad one, that concerns us all." Something in her voice made me drop into a crouch. I did not want to hear a sad message.

"Two days ago," she went on, "the king led his troops out of France after hearing that his nephew Mordred was attempting to seize the throne. As you know, he had appointed Mordred regent."

I know all too well, I thought.

"After his return, the king and Mordred met to parley, while their two armies stood in wait. But before they reached a truce, fighting broke out—"

No no no!

"There was a terrible battle, and the king was mortally wounded." Broken sobs almost drowned out her last words. "He is dead."

Now the wailing began in earnest. Rocking back and forth, I added my voice to the others, crying for Tor as well as the king. Of all the people I had ever known, they were the ones I held most dear. *Why did you leave me behind?* I thought. *What will I do now?*

The nuns began a hymn. Some folk joined in, others like me went on sobbing. I did not want to sing or even move, though the crowd around me was shifting, I stayed put. Still crouched on the floor, I caught a glimpse of feet near the altar, small ones in fine, soft, dusty red boots. Remembering the king's last words to me, I made my way to the queen and knelt before her. She put her hand on my head. "You will stay here with me, Twixt, won't you?" she asked brokenly. I told her yes.

And that is how I, once called Dungbeetle, came to live in a convent.

CHAPTER 37

When I reached him, Arthur's eyes were closed and he was scarcely breathing. A few paces away, a young man, impaled on a lance, grinned at him with blood-red teeth. Whoever he was, he had died a gruesome death after striking Arthur down.

I fell to my knees and pressed a handful of my gown against Arthur's wound. His blood quickly seeped through. Excalibur's scabbard—the one thing that could have (*should have!*) stopped the bleeding—was nowhere in sight.

A memory tugged at me, something Merlin had said when we last spoke: *However bleak the outcome, do not give up hope.*

I had puzzled over the words even as they terrified me. Now I thought, *He meant this battle. But what hope could be possible here?*

Arthur stirred, and I removed his stiff, dirt-caked gloves. His hands were warm—a good sign. I held them for a moment, then placed them on his chest. A red dragon rampant, sign of the Pendragons, was embroidered on his tunic. *Probably by Guinevere*, I thought. *Poor woman.*

Arthur's eyes opened. When he looked at me, I said, "I have failed you so badly, Arthur. Can you forgive me?"

The ghost of a smile passed over his face. "Of course," he whispered. "Don't I owe you a favor?"

I was moved beyond words that he had remembered his old, old promise, and touched my forehead to his hands. When I raised my head, a small, somber woman, richly dressed, was standing beside the body of the young man, watching me. Her dark eyes held mine for too long; then I saw the missing scabbard in her hand.

"You? You had it?" I cried, jumping to my feet. Then I thought, *Who could have stolen it but Morgan Le Fay? I should have known.*

"Here," she said, thrusting it at me. "Put it in his hands. It will keep him alive."

Yes, it will! I thought furiously, *and what incredible effrontery to tell me, its maker, what it can do!* I put the scabbard between Arthur's big, square hands, closing his fingers around it. He grasped it gently, eyes closed, and with his very next breath, his wound stopped bleeding. It was wonderful. His haggard, battle-weary face softened, his brow smoothed, and he made the sound—half sigh, half question—that a child makes when surrendering to sleep. I thought I would dissolve with relief.

Then I was flooded with such violent rage that I ran headlong at Morgan, wanting only to throw her down and kick her. But there were rillets of tears coursing down her face, framing her mouth and wetting the front of her gown. Astonished, I stopped short, my face inches from hers. I was shaking; she never even flinched.

"However cold my heart may seem to you," she said, heedless of the tears dripping off her chin, "Mordred was my nephew, and I loved him." Seeing that she meant the young man who had died attacking Arthur, I thought, *So this is Mordred.* Pelleas had mentioned him once or twice with a curtness that spelled dislike.

"How could you keep the scabbard from him?" I fairly screamed. "He is your brother! A good man and a great king! What possible reason could you have?" With the eerie sensation that I had asked her this before, the memory of Arthur's duel with Accolon came back to me. Then as now, her hatred of Arthur made no sense.

She turned her eyes on mine. They were sad, old, infinitely knowing. "You were happy with your Lake," she said, "your little . . . hideaway."

I shrank from her condescension, yet I knew she was right. My years alone at the Lake *had* been content. Those with Pelleas, brief and lovely as a summer rainbow, had been happy beyond my imagination.

"What did you want?" I asked.

"More than love," she said pointedly. "I wanted . . . dominion. And it was always just out of reach."

Dominion? I thought wonderingly. "You wanted to rule?"

"I don't expect you to understand." Her voice caught, and I thought she was going to add, *I don't even understand it myself,* an admission, however small, that she had done wrong. But for all her sorrow, Morgan was unapologetic. "Rest easy," she said, glancing at Arthur. "I no longer hate him. In fact, I mean to take him to Avalon, where he can heal."

Avalon, where only the best and most deserving spirits went, lay beyond the western horizon. It was rich in magic and always would be, no matter what happened elsewhere—or so the legend went. I only half believed; it was like one of the pretty stories that fairies were always trading. And if Avalon did exist, could I believe Morgan when she said she was taking Arthur there?

As if summoned, a black-sailed barget appeared on the ocean. Its only passenger, a tall, upright woman wearing black robes and an imposing circlet of black diamonds, stood beside a golden bier. She was as still as a sentry.

"The Queen of the Wastelands," said Morgan as the barget glided in. "A distant relation of my mother, Igraine. *Our* mother, Igraine," she amended, looking briefly at Arthur.

His face, still peaceful, was now slightly ruddy, as if he were dozing after some rigorous yet pleasant exercise. It was a hopeful sight, reminding me of Merlin and my promises. "I will go with you," I told Morgan.

"Fair enough." She spoke without surprise, as if she had known I would join her, then turned her attention to the barge. She pointed at it imperiously and her lips moved; she was spell-casting.

At her bidding the entire ocean quivered and came to rest, like an enormous creature settling down for the night.

I followed Morgan onto the barge and stationed myself next to Arthur. Watching him in repose, I felt a kind of quietude and knew my companions shared it.

Meanwhile, the barge sailed swiftly across the vast ocean, and the sun began to set—slowly at first, then with increasing speed. As it fell over the edge of the world, its very last rays found Arthur's bier, touching it with light.

And we, keeping vigil, never moved as the dark came down.

EPILOGUE

Avalon's magic is so subtle and all-pervading that any wish made here is granted at once, without the need for charms or spells. This aspect of the place is as dear to me as the excellent apples (always in season) and the bracing sea air, for whenever I long to know the fate of this person or that, I have it in a trice.

Soon after we came ashore and fell into the slow rhythms of this enchanted isle, I found myself wondering what had befallen Arthur's family, his companions, and others figuring in his wondrous life. Here is what I learned.

Margause (half sister of Morgan and Arthur, wife of King Lot, mother of Gawaine, Gaheris, Gareth, Agrivaine, and Mordred) came to a violent end. Gaheris, enraged by her affection for a young knight called Lamorek, murdered her in her bed.

❦

Lamorek's brother killed Gaheris the very same day.

❦

After losing favor at Camelot, Lancelot fled across the Narrow Sea to his lands in France. As soon as he heard of Mordred's campaign against Arthur, however, he mustered his forces and hastened back to England. He fought wholeheartedly on Arthur's behalf, and was one of the very few to survive that terrible day.

At length Lancelot found Guinevere, whom he had never ceased to love. After she sent him away (for by this time she had joined a convent), he also took holy orders and repented day and night for the rest of his life.

❦

Gawaine succumbed to an old wound on the way to Camlann, just after he and Lancelot were reconciled. He died in his old friend's arms.

❦

Guinevere narrowly avoided the ordeal of marriage to Mordred. Helped by the jester Twixt, she left court under a pretext and took refuge in a convent. Days later she was a widow. The loss of Arthur affected her deeply. After a year of mourning, Guinevere sold her magnificent jewels and built a hospice on the convent grounds. There she tended the sick and indigent—very ably, it was said—until she died.

Twixt remained with Guinevere at the convent. He lived out his days juggling for ailing children, who loved him dearly.

After leaving Merlin, Nimue roamed far and wide, gaily squandering magic. For some reason (possibly connected to a certain curse sent by a Lady who shall remain nameless), my cousin experienced a change of heart in the fastness of the world's highest mountains. There, cleansed of cruelty and greed, she learned compassion for all sentient beings and spread it so generously that she came to be worshipped as a goddess in that distant region.

Nimue's compassion eventually found its way to Merlin. It could not free him, but it did cheer him somewhat.

And Arthur? He rests here on his golden bier, safe from all harm. As the saying goes, "When the world needs him, he will return to it." Until then I will be at his side.

AUTHOR'S NOTE

Damosel began long ago, with an image—a woman's hand rising out of a lake, brandishing a sword. When I first saw it, in an illustrated book about King Arthur, it seemed beautiful and mysterious, even a touch sinister, and it made me want to read the book right away—not so much because I liked knights in armor, but because I wanted answers to all the questions the image raised: Whose sword was it? Why was a woman holding it? (Women didn't have swords, did they?) Why was she underwater? Could she breathe down there?

In this way, at the age of nine or so, I met the Lady of the Lake.

Years later, when I read Sir Thomas Malory's *Le Morte d'Arthur*, the Lady reappeared, and now she was even more of an enigma. In Malory's great book (written in the fifteenth century and the source of most Arthurian fiction), the Lady's behavior was so inconsistent that she seemed like the victim of violent mood swings. In one episode she was vengeful, in another scheming, seductive, and cruel (Malory has her seducing and betraying Merlin), but then, in a third, wonderfully benevolent. Behaving very much like a fairy godmother, she saved Arthur's life on three occasions.

Because most of the other characters in the Arthurian stories are either full of virtue or very, very bad, the Lady's ambiguity is striking. Or at least it was to me.

A story about her began to form in my mind, one that gave interesting (if not plausible) reasons for her strange behavior. I found myself imagining her world, which (based on Malory and the French Arthurian romances, and many other works of fiction about Arthur) was in flux, with magic fading and Christianity on the rise. They coexisted peacefully, if briefly: this was long before magic was considered the devil's work.

At the same time (and now I was back in the real world, reading nonfiction about life in the British Isles after nearly four hundred years of Roman occupation), a brilliant military strategist, a native Briton, had managed to subdue the many kings and warlords seeking power after the Romans sailed home. He united them and ruled them, and for one shining moment, peace prevailed. Historians seem to think that if King Arthur did exist (and there is endless debate on the subject), he may well have been that remarkable man.

Not much is known about the fifth century in England. Life was harsh, with few amenities. Most of the population was illiterate. Roman baths, bridges, and roads endured (they were very well built, after all), but much else, including the once-great city of Londinium, rapidly fell into decline. Needless to say, this was long before knights had shining armor—they were lucky if they had armor at all.

By now I had decided that I would actually write a book about the Lady of the Lake, and setting it much earlier than the fifteenth century (when most Arthurian stories take place, thanks to Malory) made sense to me. A murky, primitive time like the fifth century, when Christianity did in fact take hold in Britain, was perfect for a story about the disappearance of magic.

So now, with something resembling a historical context, I went back to *Le Morte d'Arthur* and read the passages about the Lady of the Lake very carefully. As I mentioned, in that book she is both bad and good. I chose to believe that she was good, if flawed, and would never dream of harming Merlin, so I invented Nimue. I also wanted to show her emerging from seclusion and falling in love, so I expanded on the story of Pelleas. And because there is no reason given in *Le Morte d'Arthur* for the Lady's extended absence from Camelot, I made it a period of mourning.

Finally, dwarves do appear in the early Arthurian tales—they pop up suddenly, usually to deliver a message, and then vanish. While I did research for *Damosel*, I began to imagine a dwarf who did not vanish, but remained, to play a significant part in the narrative. And why not? Unlike Damosel, he could be close to Arthur and Guinevere, and because he was at court, he could witness Camelot's demise at first hand. That said, once I began writing about Twixt, his role changed and grew. As someone who has always been skeptical when a writer claims that a character "took over" a story, I found myself experiencing precisely that with Twixt. I introduced him and he proceeded to live his own (turbulent) life. I can't say I minded—by the time I finished the book, I was very fond of him.

In fact, by that time I was fond of *all* the characters— Excalibur, Ralphus, the birds, the gnomes, the royals, the knights, even the many villains—and left their world of fading magic knowing I would miss it.

I tell myself I can always go back.

Stephanie Spinner is the author of the novels *Quiver*, a retelling of the Greek myth of Atalanta, and *Quicksilver*, the story of Hermes, fleet-footed messenger to the Olympian gods. She's written many other books for young readers, including *Aliens for Breakfast* with Jonathan Etra; *It's a Miracle! A Hanukkah Storybook*, illustrated by Jill McElmurry; and an adaptation of *The Nutcracker*, illustrated by Peter Malone.

After a distinguished career in children's book publishing, Stephanie Spinner now writes full-time from her home in Connecticut. To learn more about the author and her books, please visit www.stephaniespinner.com.